RUNNING MATES

Carole reached for the scarf, but Steve jerked it away playfully. When she lunged at him, Steve grabbed her arms and pinned them behind her. "You give?" he challenged her, grinning uncontrollably.

"Never!" Carole fought like a wildcat, but Steve was too strong for her. As she thrashed to get away, Carole was suddenly aware of a feeling she'd never had before. There was a new thrill in this closeness, a sense that they belonged like this, laughing and happy together. Still, she wouldn't let herself relax and give up. No matter how she felt, she couldn't let him win.

"You're really something, you know that?" Steve whispered. "A worthy adversary."

"Yeah," she mumbled, her dark eyes fixed on his. "You're not so bad yourself."

Bantam Sweet Dreams Romances
Ask your bookseller for the books you have missed

Running Mates

Jocelyn Saal

BANTAM BOOKS
TORONTO · NEW YORK · LONDON · SYDNEY

RL 6, Il age 11 and up

RUNNING MATES
A Bantam Book / May 1983

Cover photo by Pat Hill

ISBN 0-553-23341-6

Published simultaneously in the United States and Canada

PRINTED IN THE UNITED STATES OF AMERICA

O   0 9 8 7 6 5 4 3 2 1

*To the poor and rich,
the old and young,
the black and white of our country.
Together we exemplify
the power of the vote.*

Chapter One

We'll take a cup of kindness yet,
For auld lang syne!

Raucous voices rang in the New Year, and people began running around the living room, kissing one another gleefully. Only Carole stayed where she was, strumming her guitar in the corner. Being the accompanist was a good excuse since she didn't feel much like celebrating.

"Sweetheart!" Her mother came over and planted a noisy kiss on Carole's lustrous, long, dark hair. "How about the eats and drinks? Go on and help Mary Ann. And—happy New Year!"

"Same to you, Mom." Carole nodded, balancing her guitar carefully against the wall and starting toward the Baileys' kitchen. She thought this party was a bit strange—adults and kids all together—but the food was a welcome break from all the good cheer that she wasn't in the mood for sharing.

Mary Ann Bailey was standing alone in the kitchen, licking guacamole dip off her fingers. Carole sidled up beside her friend and poked her in the ribs.

"Yow! What the—? Carole Weiss, for goodness sake! Don't start acting like my thirteen-year-old brother!" She took one last lick and began setting crackers around the bowl of dip.

"How's it going?" Carole asked, staring at the gigantic buffet Mrs. Bailey had prepared with Mary Ann and Carole's help. They had decided to be terribly chic and save their feast until after midnight.

"I'm having a good time. Everything's just fine, except for the music." Carole nodded, perching herself on top of the counter. "Bor-*ring*, is what I'd call it." She sighed and popped a piece of salami into her mouth.

"Well, what do you expect? Our folks are not about to listen to the Police or the Clash."

"But that's the point," Carole said, raising her voice over the racket in the other room. The adults had just cracked open a bottle of champagne. "What are we doing here? New Year's Eve with our parents and your brother! Come on, MA."

Mary Ann shrugged and ran her fingers through her silky red hair. "Hey, this is Hartford, Connecticut. What else were we supposed o do without dates? I don't think most places ven let you in unaccompanied."

"Well, I think that's criminal," Carole stated mphatically. She eyed the Swedish meatballs nungrily and then speared one with a tooth-pick. "Is there a law on the books that says it's ill got to be like in the old days, girls protected rom life by guys, girls walking down the street on the inside so the guy gets splashed by the street sweeper? Not that they don't deserve it," she added, smirking. There was a decided twin-kle in her dark brown eyes.

"You've still got it bad, don't you?" Mary Ann asked her softly.

"What are you talking about?" Carole frowned.

"Steve Landy, of course. Wasn't it—? Oh! It was last New Year's Eve that you broke up! Hey, I'm sorry, Carole. I didn't remember." She came over to hug her friend, but Carole just laughed.

"You can't really think I'm still pining for that guy, MA. You must know me better than that."

She sounded pretty convincing, even to her own ears. It had been a whole year, and natu-rally time heals all wounds. She'd only been a stupid sophomore when she was nuts about Steve, and now, halfway through junior year, she'd seen just how wrong she had been about him. Steve was a big, tall bore, not to mention being filled to the brim with zillions of old-fashioned ideas about men and women and life in general. Basically, Steve was just a male chau-

3

vinist. He thought girls were weaker than guys and that they couldn't compete in sports with guys because they'd be at a disadvantage. He thought girls were born with a bad sense of direction and an inferior ability to do math. What *didn't* he think?! Actually, as Carole looked back on their relationship, she couldn't remember one measly topic, from pizza toppings to nuclear disarmament, on which they had ever agreed. Their time together was spent in pitched battles, where Steve was always calm and sure of his opinions and Carole was flustered though equally vehement.

She sighed and abandoned the meatballs for a fudge brownie.

"You're thinking awfully hard about something," Mary Ann observed, lining up dishes on a long tray.

"Do you know what he said to me once? Do you know what really clinched it?"

"What?"

Carole shook her head in amazement. "Steve Landy had the nerve, the bold-faced nerve, to state that there would never be a woman president of the United States. Can you believe that?" She munched the brownie with a hungry vengeance.

"He's stupid." Mary Ann shrugged.

"He's not," Carole objected. "He's terribly smart. He's just thick and dense and—"

"I thought you hadn't bothered giving him a

moment's consideration for a year." Her friend smiled wisely. "What's going on?"

"Oh!" Carole swung off the counter. "It's New Year's Eve, all right? I'm entitled to be a little depressed. You know what everybody says about how awful the holidays can be, if you're not in the right mood. And this one is the worst!" She marched over to help her friend lift the heavy tray, but then she got sidetracked by another thought, as she often did.

"It seems to me that I was very immature last year," she said. "Totally wrapped up in being the model high-school sophomore. But you know what Dave always says?"

"No, tell me, what *does* Dave always say?" Mary Ann laughed. Dave Lasker, another junior, was Carole's favorite source of wisdom.

"He says there's no fool like a young fool."

"Well, he ought to know." Mary Ann jerked her head at the tray, and together they brought it to the dining room, which had been set up buffet-style. The adults were gathered around the TV watching lots of girls in sequined leotards dancing around a gigantic cake.

"The food! Hooray!" yelled Tommy Bailey, Mary Ann's kid brother. He'd been running around the house like a banshee, much to his mother's dismay. But after all, it wasn't every night he got to stay up with the adults. "I want champagne!" he shouted.

"Well, you can't have any," Mary Ann said emphatically.

"I want it!"

"Mary Ann . . ." Her mother stood at the doorway and looked at her pleadingly.

"I know." Carole grinned. "How about having Mary Ann's special lemonade, instead?"

"Yeah, Tommy." Mary Ann smiled knowingly. "I'll make you my terrific, wonderful lemonade." Her mother went back to the living room, and Mary Ann ran into the kitchen for the ingredients, while Carole hung back, thinking of the last time her friend had played this little trick.

"Hey, here you go!" Mary Ann sat her brother down and put a glass in front of him, at the very edge of the table. "A glass of club soda, a nice juicy lemon, and two packets of Sweet 'n Low."

Her brother frowned. "I want sugar."

"No, it's better with Sweet 'n Low, believe me." Mary Ann squeezed the lemon into the bubbly water and tore open the two packets. "Ready?" she asked.

"Ready," Tommy answered. Carole shook her head in amusement. Mary Ann had done this at a party last year, and it was the hit of the evening. Steve was the only one who hadn't appreciated her practical joke.

Mary Ann dumped both packets in at once. The mixture began to bubble madly, half the glass already churning and dancing. Then, the entire thing rose over the top of the glass and poured into Tommy's lap. He was soaked.

"Hey!" he complained. Then he started laughing hysterically.

"Sugar doesn't do that, so I had to use Sweet 'n Low," his sister said, giggling as she mopped him up with paper towels.

"Real funny, MA," Carole drawled. She remembered she'd been snuggling in the corner with Steve when Mary Ann had pulled that one. She was so short—barely five feet—and Steve was so tall, that she was getting a crick in her neck from leaning up to look at him. But it was pretty nice, aside from that. Then Mary Ann had come over and offered them some lemonade—and had made Steve hold the glass. Steve had looked as if he would explode, no matter how often Carole explained that her friend was just a dedicated practical joker.

"Can I try it out on Mom?" Tommy begged the girls, just as the adults came into the dining room to help themselves to the food.

"Not tonight, tiger," Carole cautioned him.

"Yeah, OK. Guess I'll lie down for a bit, then," he said, fanning his wet clothes. "Just for a minute." He flopped down on the couch in the living room, and in a moment he was asleep.

Their parents were exclaiming over the silly antics of the TV emcee, so Carole and Mary Ann grabbed two Cokes, filled a plate with some dip and chips, and retreated back into the kitchen.

7

"Happy New Year," Carole said, shrugging and raising her can in a toast.

"Happy junior year," Mary Ann countered. "Hey, if it's not too painful, why don't you tell me what you two did last New Year's? I'm absolutely pining for a night on the town with a guy. Even just talking about one would make me feel better. That is, I mean, if it isn't too painful."

"Painful!" Carole snorted. "Listen, what was painful was listening to all of Steve's old-fashioned ideas day in and day out. Even New Year's. See, we were going to this party in some big house in West Hartford—"

"Fancy neighborhood!" Mary Ann interrupted.

"You said it. Some friends of his folks, I guess. Anyhow, I had on a really nice pair of jeans and a frilly blouse when he met me at the door. He told me—get this—he told me to put on a dress!"

"What for?" Mary Ann glanced down at her own jeans.

"He was wearing a suit and tie. I don't know, that's what started the whole thing. We sat in his car and argued about how different we were."

Mary Ann giggled. "You don't have to argue about something as obvious as that."

"Yeah, right. But he kept saying I just did things to be different, to stand out in a crowd. And I said he just acted conservative on purpose, to stand out in a crowd."

"Sounds like the two of you have more in

common than I thought," Mary Ann said, laughing. She was about to say something else, when the door swung open. Carole's mother stood there, hands on her hips.

"You girls! Why don't you come in and join the festivities?" Mrs. Weiss asked. "They're almost over, and we'll be going home before too long, Carole."

"OK, Mom. We'll be right with you."

Mrs. Weiss gave them an understanding look, then popped back through the swinging doors into the living room.

"I hate it when she does that," Carole whispered, going to the refrigerator for another Coke.

"Does what?" Mary Ann asked.

"Oh, she looks at me all sad-eyed, like she's sorry for me not having a boyfriend. I mean, what's the big deal?"

"I guess when you're a mother you think that your daughter should be dating constantly," Mary Ann suggested.

Carole frowned and thought for a minute. "No, I think it's more that she doesn't like me spending time alone. She thinks it's weird. A lot she knows!" Carole gave her friend a silly little grin.

"Yeah. Being alone's real important. You learn a lot about yourself," Mary Ann said philosophically. "And to be honest, Carole, I think you're a much nicer person since you broke up with

Steve. Much more mature and a really good friend."

"Thanks." Carole smiled, taking Mary Ann's hand and giving it a squeeze. "I was hoping you felt that way."

Carole broke away with a laugh. "This is much too serious for New Year's Eve. Let's go join the crowd, shall we?"

"But we haven't made our resolutions," Mary Ann said, stopping her friend at the kitchen door. "I vow to play the stereo one notch lower and to be good to my little brother—at least some of the time. How about you?"

Carole flipped her thick hair out of her eyes and made a serious face. "I vow to be true to myself, to preserve my integrity in the face of the foolishness around me, and not to care what other people say behind my back."

"Pretty heavy-duty."

"Yeah. C'mon, let's go back to the grown-ups, OK?"

They pushed the door open and marched to the living room, both of them realizing that although this wasn't the best New Year's Eve either of them had ever spent, it wasn't the worst, either. The only problem with the evening, Carole thought, as she retreated to her corner and picked up her guitar again, was that it was hard not to be inhibited in front of adults. She and Mary Ann could never act the same with their parents as they did around each other.

She began strumming Kim Carnes's "Bette Davis Eyes" softly, because Tommy was still asleep on the other side of the room. She tuned out the adults' conversation about politics and the economy, and she tried to concentrate on the major subject of the evening—her New Year's resolutions.

They really made sense. They all had to do with being alone and independent and with what you did or didn't do. During the months she'd been going out with Steve, Carole had had a little voice in the back of her mind that was continually whispering, "You're copping out. Stick up for yourself!" Steve was just like a grown-up, full of conservative opinions that were even less convincing because he was really only a dumb teenager. But Carole had trouble arguing with him, since he always took the accepted point of view—one accepted by forty-year-olds at any rate.

And what was this big to-do about boys, anyway? she mused, switching keys and picking out the melody to "I Got the Beat." Boys were status symbols, and that was the only thing they were good for. It was easy to have long talks into the night with another girl, and also very satisfying, since ideas could be exchanged. Boys, on the other hand, loved to hear themselves talk and took every opportunity to ramble on incessantly. They were show-offs, as Carole saw it, even Dave, who was a friend as opposed to a boyfriend. He just liked to exhibit his smarts, of which he had plenty.

Then there was the physical side. Now here it was more complicated because there was no way to get around that tingly feeling that comes from kissing a special boy. It was like putting on a new outfit and peering into the mirror and seeing for yourself that you really weren't half bad-looking. Steve made her feel that way. All she had to do was look at him, or catch him looking at her out of the corner of his eye, and she would melt. Kissing Steve was almost literally a pain in the neck, but it was worth it.

Carole sighed and glanced over at Mary Ann, who was passing around a tray of fancy cookies and behaving like a good, model teenager for the benefit of the Weisses and the Baileys. Little did they know the true MA, the raving weirdo under that mature exterior, who emerged to play practical jokes when no adults were present. Carole couldn't help envying her friend a little for adapting so well. Mary Ann could slip in and out of two worlds like a chameleon changing color. Of course, the practical-joking side was the real MA, at least at this point in her life. No guy had ever gone out with her more than twice, because she had always pulled some hilarious trick on him, and that discouraged all romance. Carole had told her she was denying her true feelings, but Mary Ann said she'd never had true feelings for any guy. She'd know when she did, and then she wouldn't play jokes anymore.

Carole's own feelings were awfully confused. She hadn't thought seriously about Steve in months, and now, just because this was the anniversary of their breakup, here she was, totally bummed out. The odd thing was, she hadn't ever considered getting back together with him— he was the one who used to get all dreamy-eyed every time he saw her in the cafeteria or the hallway at school. It was funny, but as far as she knew, he had hardly dated since the second half of sophomore year. Still, Carole was sure that by now Steve had stopped caring for her.

"Sweetheart." Her mother's voice roused her from her thoughts. "Would you play that nice Beatles' song you learned? Then we've really got to go." She gave Carole's father an insistent look.

"Sure, Mom." Carole took a breath and swung into "Yesterday." Funny how music could change her mood so quickly. When she played something bouncy and light, she felt that way herself. When she played a slow, sad song, her whole being quieted down, and her thoughts turned inward.

This song did that to her. All evening long she'd been complaining about Steve, telling MA what a jerk he was, how he didn't respect women as individuals, blah, blah, blah. But suddenly she started remembering all the good things about him. His warm, lovely smile that made his eyes two crinkly brown dots under his shock of chestnut hair. His long, stringy legs, running crazily for a bus. His deep, musical voice. The way he always, unfailingly, took Carole's arm when they crossed a street. She remembered the bicycle trip they had taken with a bunch of kids the summer before last—zipping along the streets together, sometimes holding hands to show the others how good they were. All he had to do was look at her, and they would both know exactly what the other was thinking. Even when they had just been fighting like cats and dogs, that look always got to her. It was Steve's way of saying he cared for her very much, despite their differences. And although he never actually said the words, she sensed how special she was to him.

Well, he wasn't all bad, she decided. And if he wasn't a guy she'd once felt strongly about, she might actually consider getting together with him just as friends. She kind of enjoyed their arguments—they got her blood stirring and her adrenaline pumping. No other boy had ever done that to her.

Except by now, too much time had passed. A whole year had changed them both, and they were virtually strangers. They hadn't talked about their summer vacations or about their grades or about school events or what senior year would be like. Carole had the music club and her crowd; Steve was all involved in school politics, since he was head of the debating team and on zillions of committees. They were worlds apart.

The grown-ups and Mary Ann hummed softly as Carole played the end of the song. Then everyone was quiet, deep in private thoughts.

"Well." Mr. Weiss finally broke the silence. "I guess it's time to say good night."

He stood up, and Mrs. Bailey went to get the coats. Carole started packing up her guitar. She wanted to say, "Why can't we all stay here and put another log on the fire and watch the sun come up?" But she didn't think her idea would go over very well with the adults.

Mrs. Bailey handed everyone their coats, and Mary Ann put an arm around Carole's shoulder, while the parents all said good night. "Listen, thanks for helping out."

"My pleasure," Carole said, grinning and stuffing her hair under her purple ski hat.

"It wasn't as bad as we expected, right?" Mary Ann whispered.

"No . . . I had fun." Carole hugged her friend, then thanked the Baileys. Tommy was still curled up on the couch.

"It's going to be a great year—I just know it," Mrs. Weiss was saying as she wrapped herself in her down coat.

"Right on the money," Mr. Weiss agreed.

Carole walked out into the deep snow behind

15

her parents. She felt that it was going to be her year, to mess up or fix up at will. She could do whatever she pleased with it, maybe even change it for the better.

"Hey, Carole!" Mary Ann yelled from the door.

Carole turned around, just in time to catch a large, fluffy snowball right in the face.

"I'll get you," she jokingly threatened as she walked backward toward their car. "And you know I always win!"

Chapter Two

"And in terms of the position of Twain High in the community, we see the ultimate responsibility lying on our shoulders."

Dave Lasker, editor-in-chief of the *Herald*, smacked his copy down on the desk. "What do you think?"

Carole frowned and leaned forward, taking the piece of paper from him. The big basement room that served as headquarters for the school paper was alive with the clicks of typewriter keys. The newsroom was a room no one wanted for anything else. It was at the end of a long basement corridor in back of the boiler room and had once been used for storage. Even after the kids had cleaned it up, a lot of junk still remained. There was an old megaphone, discarded by the football team, a partial set of golf clubs, and telephone books going back to the year one. One of Dave's favorite rumors was

17

that the first principal of Twain High was buried inside one of the walls, but he couldn't convince anyone of that.

Carole loved the room. To her it smelled of creativity and energy. The first semester she had been a reporter on the paper, but she had found that it interfered with her music, so she had quit. She still helped Dave, however, by going over his editorials and by writing occasional articles when he was short-staffed. As she examined Dave's editorial, she frowned and shook her head.

"Well?" he demanded.

"Too routine for you," she finally commented after skimming the page. "And I don't like 'lying on our shoulders.' It's a cliché."

"Horsefeathers!" Dave Lasker stood up so violently he nearly knocked his chair over. He was a skinny, wiry kid, whose head of dark blond hair was the biggest part of him. He had small but intelligent eyes and very white skin. He said he shunned the sun because it sapped the brain. "You've been down on me for weeks, Carole," he said in a hurt tone of voice.

"Dave, you always told me you liked me to go over your stuff. Please don't start getting all sensitive about it now."

"You got any bright ideas on how to change it?" he asked grudgingly, sitting down again. Much as he hated to admit it, he knew she was right.

"Look." She edged over beside him. "The point of the piece is that we need volunteers for the elementary school lunch program, right?"

"Because some of their parents can't afford to pay for it. Exactly! And somebody else ought to chip in if they can't." He pounded his fist on the desk.

"You're too emotional about it," Carole said. She pointed at his second paragraph. "This is all a lot of high-flown rhetoric—you get too wordy."

"Listen, you cluck, the bigger my ideas, the more I have to say about them. I want people to sit up and take notice." When she didn't say anything, he shrugged, and his serious face creased into a smile. "Go on, go ahead with the critique." He sighed. "I'll take it like a man."

Carole rubbed her forehead. "This isn't journalism to you; it's a cause. I don't see why you wanted to be editor-in-chief in the first place."

"Because I'm too short to play basketball," he said, grimacing. "Are you going to help me with this, or what?"

At that moment the door of the newsroom opened, and in walked the last person in the world Carole wanted to see. Steve Landy.

"Uh, hi, Dave. Hi, Sylvie," he said to a skinny girl who was working the Xerox machine beside the door. "How're you, Pat?" He made the rounds of the large room, and only after he had greeted everyone else did he give Carole a perfunctory

19

hello. When he did, he turned beet red under his fair skin.

"How're you doing?" she asked casually, staring down at Dave's editorial as though her life depended on it.

"How may we be of service?" Dave asked, in his "are you putting me on?" voice.

"Well, I. . . ." Steve looked around for a chair in which he could rest his lanky frame, but there were none available. He finally leaned one hip on the side of the desk nearest to Carole. "I was talking to your adviser, Mr. Schlesinger, and he happened to mention that you had some ideas about covering the senior class elections. I just wanted to go over a few things." He was speaking to Dave, but his eyes kept wandering off toward Carole. She just ignored him, putting her red pencil to Dave's article with fierce determination.

"Are you running for senior class president?" Dave finally plucked the pencil from Carole's hand and pulled his editorial back, putting it into a folder.

"I guess so." Steve chuckled. "I do have leadership experience."

"Yeah, and so did Napoleon." Carole snickered. Dave thought that was pretty funny, and he doubled over with laughter, but when Carole saw the hurt look on Steve's face, she immediately regretted her gibe.

"What are you guys thinking about doing?" Steve rushed on.

"Well, I want to call a couple of press conferences," Dave answered seriously. "And we'll print in-depth profiles of the candidates a couple of weeks before the election. I might even get Carole here to join up for the election committee. In case I need an article from the committee point of view."

"That's a great idea," Steve said.

"Now wait a second! I'm not a political writer. I never said—" Carole sputtered. If she got involved in the election, that practically guaranteed she'd have to sit around with Steve for an afternoon or two or three. No telling where that could lead, and she didn't want things between Steve and her to go *anywhere.*

"I don't want any back talk from you!" Dave emphasized each word by banging his fist on the table. Then he turned back to Steve. "I guess I'll rev the thing up in about a month, when all the candidates are announced. Who's planning to knock you off your perch, Landy?" he questioned, giving Steve a playful smile.

"I might give it a shot," a high voice piped up from the doorway. They all turned to see Sally Scott, head of the junior class entertainment committee. She aced every course and was generally considered to be a grind, although she seemed to make time for an astounding number of extracurricular activities. Carole thought

Sally was about the dullest person she'd ever met, and she couldn't get over her clothes. She wore pearls to school, for Pete's sake! And she never wore pants or jeans, even in the coldest weather. Her skirts were always perfectly ironed, as if she never sat down in them. Her shoulder-length blond hair was turned under at what seemed to be forty-five degrees all around, and her light eyelashes blinked furiously whenever she talked, which was nearly all the time. There was nothing really bad about Sally that Carole could put her finger on—it was just that she was another grown-up in disguise and, therefore, the enemy.

"Are you running, too, Scott?" Dave asked, whipping out the small note pad that was as much a part of him as his navy baseball cap, which he wore in every season and every kind of weather. "What's your platform?"

Sally smiled her "I know something you don't know" smile, which never failed to drive Carole crazy. "Later for that. I just came in to place an ad. My father has decided our little newspaper is worthy of endorsement." Sally's father owned a very successful restaurant in West Hartford and certainly didn't need to advertise in Twain High's insignificant paper. Carole caught a glimpse of Steve's expression, and even *he* seemed to be annoyed that Sally would use such a cheap political trick.

"It's interesting," Steve murmured as they

watched Sally stride over to Pat Taylor, who was in charge of advertising, "how everybody scratches everybody else's back when it comes down to the crunch. Life is politics, you know," he said.

"Yeah, well, what about you, Landy?" Dave probed, writing furiously in his notebook. "You've been, let's see—freshman year you were a big shot in the photography club, sophomore year you got on the debating team, and this year, you were elected its president, not to mention all that committee work you do in your spare time. You must want senior class president pretty bad."

Carole was getting uncomfortable. First of all, she felt really out of it with all this discussion of political maneuvers and who would do what for whom to get ahead. And besides that, she didn't like Dave putting Steve on the defensive—even though Steve seemed to be getting a kick out of it. She could tell that the very thought of running against Sally had him all psyched up. She wouldn't really describe Steve as competitive, but he sure hated to lose. Suddenly Carole felt very protective of him. And she didn't like that feeling—at all.

"Well, I guess I'll shove off," she muttered, pushing her chair back. "Got to tackle that algebra homework. See you." She waved.

"Carole, wait up, I'll walk you," Dave said, tucking his pad in his back jeans pocket and grabbing an oversized manila envelope. "I've got to run the dummy over to the printer." Then he turned to Steve and smirked. "I haven't finished with you yet, buster. Be prepared to squirm under my interrogation."

Steve gave him a sweeping bow. "I look forward to it, and to having you as one of my constituents."

"*Me!*" Dave hooted. "You gotta be kidding! And just because you came to me before any of the other candidates doesn't mean you have an edge on anyone else. Remember that."

"Hey, I'll just give you the facts, I promise," Steve assured him, watching as Dave and Carole made their way to the door of the newsroom. Carole had her hand on the knob when she heard Steve say, "I'll sit still for that profile, Dave, but only if you can persuade Carole to sign up for the election committee." He turned to her. "What about it?"

"Nope—no, thanks. I really want to spend more time on my music this semester."

Dave gave her a thump on the back. "Are you gonna start that rock band you keep talking about? I'm terrific—I keep telling you! What do you say you let me pound the drums?"

"We'll see," she said, grinning, then turned back to Steve. "So you see, I'm afraid I'll be too busy to get very involved in the election." She smiled sweetly, trying not to think too hard about how good he looked, with his olive corduroy jacket

24

hanging open over his black jeans. He seemed awfully interested in her getting into school politics. Now what did *that* mean?

"Carole." Steve walked over and drew her away from Dave, who looked immediately suspicious. "The election is really important. A lot hinges on it. Think about spending your entire senior year under a corrupt or lackluster government. You want the best for yourself and your fellow classmates, don't you?" He was talking very seriously, as if he were running for US Senate and Carole were the decisive vote that would keep the country out of war.

"Sorry, Steve," she said quietly. "My algebra calls. Oh, say, I left my guitar up in the music room, Dave. Got to go pick it up."

Dave shrugged and stepped into the corridor. She was about to follow, when Steve grabbed her by the elbow and closed the door to the newsroom, leaving Dave standing outside.

"Please think about it. You can start your rock band as soon as the final vote is tallied. But your participation is really important, Carole, believe me." His deep brown eyes were so earnest, so determined. She looked up into them with her own fierce brand of conviction.

"Why is this such an issue?" she asked, withdrawing her arm from his grasp. "There are plenty of other people to do committee stuff. I don't see why you need me."

"Because. Because Twain High needs the best

brains, the people who really get in there and work."

He seemed so determined about this that she had to stop for a second and think about it. Besides, she was really quite flattered at the high opinion he seemed to have of her abilities. Maybe she should reconsider. "We'll see," she told him after a second. "I'll give it some thought."

"Please do," he said, opening the door for her. Dave was standing on the other side with his ear practically to the door.

"You two finished with the summit conference?" he asked, without the slightest bit of embarrassment.

"We have just begun." Steve smiled. Then he gave a little wave and walked off, as Carole stood staring after him. Her mind flashed back to her New Year's resolutions, and she took a deep breath.

"What's with *him*?" Dave asked, starting off in the opposite direction.

"I don't know."

"You don't, huh? I think you *do*," he said, laughing.

"What do you mean?" Carole hurried after him and caught up as he approached the stairwell.

"You don't think Mr. Cool there is really concerned about losing to Sally Scott or anybody else who decides to run, do you? It seems to me that, just possibly, he intends to wheedle himself into your good graces in order to get the election committee on his side. C'mon, Weiss—" Dave poked her in the ribs. " 'Fess up, now. Tell Dave all about it."

Carole gave him a look. "I don't know what you're talking about."

"No. Of course, you don't. You don't know anything about going out with Landy last year and smooching in corners."

"That was a year ago, Dave. Besides," she added, storming up the steps toward the second floor, "Steve is simply not the kind of person who'd use a personal relationship to get himself special favors. One thing the guy has is political savvy. He needs me like a hole in the head." She shrugged and walked ahead to the music room.

"Horsefeathers," Dave exclaimed, coming up behind her. "You're full of hot air, Weiss, and that guy's got your number. So help me, even if I did vote, I wouldn't give him half a ballot."

Carole turned and shook a finger in Dave's face. "You of all people, you bleeding-heart editorial writer, ought to know it's your civic duty to participate in the electoral process. And you also ought to give more credit to an honest, hard-working candidate. Steve Landy is perfectly qualified to be president of the senior class," she said as she walked inside the music room and took her guitar from a corner.

"You've got it bad, kid," Dave said, laughing,

and Carole whirled around, furious, recognizing that this was exactly what Mary Ann had accused her of on New Year's Eve.

"Let me alone, will you?" She didn't want to think about why she was suddenly so angry. "Listen, I meant what I said. I don't want anything to do with that election. I don't want to be on the committee, I don't want to go to press conferences, I don't even want to go to the inaugural ball, for heaven's sake!"

"Carole, you're yelling," Dave teased, ushering her out the door. "C'mon with me to the printer," he suggested. "I want some company."

She sighed and walked behind him down the hall. It was already getting dark outside, and Carole felt her mood slipping into the same drab grayness as the winter weather. They walked to their lockers in silence to get their coats and books.

As they were standing on the top step of the school, buttoning up against the biting cold wind, Dave said, "You convinced me. I'm going to do my civic duty."

"Oh, really?" Carole looked skeptical. "What civic duty are you referring to?" She switched her guitar case into her left hand and bent her head into the wind.

"I'm going to vote. Yes, I will exercise my right," Dave declared. "I'm gonna vote for Sally."

"You—! Oh, come on, Dave, be serious."

"I am. I think it's time your friend Landy had

28

an upset. Here, we can take the Asylum Avenue bus to Sigourney." He started jogging toward the stop on the corner.

"But, Sally, she's . . . she's so unimaginative," Carole complained, panting after him. "She's a plodder. I think she'd make a lousy president."

"And why would Landy make a better one?" Dave waved the bus down and charged up the steps as soon as the doors swung open.

"I already told you." Carole moved to the back of the bus, squeezing past some people to get to an open standing place. "Experience, good relationships with faculty and students, ability to see different sides of an issue—well, he's been on the debating team, after all." She smiled to herself, thinking back to the time when she and Steve had been together. He sure couldn't see different sides of the issues that *they* had argued about. "Also, he wants the job—even more than Sally, I bet."

"Exactly what I thought." Dave started laughing, causing several of the passengers to stare at him. "I knew if I hounded you long enough, you'd come out with the truth."

"What?" Carole peered out the window to see the street sign.

"Spoken like a true advocate. You ought to be his campaign manager." Dave chuckled.

"I'd like to change the subject." Carole glared at him, wishing he would turn off those penetrating eyes that saw right through her to her motives and dreams. Dave was uncanny that way. Sometimes he knew what she was thinking before she even knew it herself.

"Sure, that's cool." Dave nodded.

They started talking about other things, and when it was time to get off, Carole followed Dave out onto the avenue, telling herself not to pay any attention to his teasing. When she and Steve had just broken up, all she got from friends and family were sympathetic looks and smiles, as if some sort of tragedy had occurred. As the months passed, though, their concern had turned to amusement. For the life of her she didn't know why. They acted as if she were fooling herself, as if she really did want to get back together with Steve but was just playing hard to get. The boys who asked her out on dates implied by hinting or even saying it aloud, that she was still Steve Landy's girl. That was why, exasperated and disgusted with them all, Carole had stopped dating about six months before. Being alone was infinitely better than having to listen to all those dumb assumptions. But now it was probably too late for her to get Steve back, even if she had wanted to.

"Here we are." Dave swung open the door of Creative Printing and ushered Carole inside. Mr. Graffman, the owner, a big, red-faced man with a bald head and a large belly, was leaning over the pile of invoices on his desk, scratching his head and muttering to himself.

"Hi, Mr. Graffman." Dave smiled, handing him the large manila envelope. "Under the wire again, but we made it."

Mr. Graffman eased his glasses up on his forehead. "And I suppose you want the job done overnight, Davie, am I right?"

Carole and Dave exchanged looks. They were used to the printer's world-weary attitude. They just wished he'd get their names straight.

"As soon as possible," Dave said, whipping the top sheet off Mr. Graffman's work-order pad and starting to fill it out.

"Dave's going to have more material than he knows what to do with for the next couple of issues," Carole told Mr. Graffman. "Senior class election's coming up, you know." She peered into the back, where the noise and rumble of the presses was like the distant roar of a great beast huddling into its cave. She and Dave really loved this place—the smell of the ink, the rhythm of the typesetting machines, the flow of papers coming off the presses.

"I admire what you're doing, kids," Mr. Graffman said, flipping through the page dummies as he always did. "Just a few years ago, kids were nuts, they were crazy. Hanging out on the streets playing their radios, getting into trouble. Not like you kids."

Dave looked at the floor, and Carole almost burst out laughing. There were more than a few at Twain High who matched Mr. Graffman's description.

"So, ah, you think maybe next Tuesday, Mr. Graffman?" Dave asked hopefully.

"Davie, Carolyn," the printer said loudly. "You keep writing, keep thinking. That's what makes a democracy function. Either of you running for office in this election?"

"Me?!" Dave shrieked with laughter. "Kissing babies is not my thing," he declared.

"We've got a couple of good candidates lined up, though," Carole assured him. "Kids who really care about the senior class, the school, and the community."

"I like that, I really do." Mr. Graffman's red face got even redder with pleasure. "Bring them around, I'd like to meet them. Davie, for you, I'll make it Tuesday," he said, ripping off the back carbon of the work order. "But you know," he added, just as they started for the door, "Twain High couldn't do any better than one of you two kids. If you don't mind my saying so, you give the neighborhood a good name."

"Thanks, Mr. Graffman," Carole said, pushing the door open. "Goodbye."

And right at that moment, something started changing inside her. First Steve, then Mr. Graffman, had suggested that the way to get good government was to get good people. If she just sat back and took things easy and started her rock group, nothing really terrible would happen to Twain High's senior class. But maybe the best wouldn't happen either.

"See you Tuesday," Dave called over his shoulder, closing the door behind them. "Whew!" he breathed, hurrying down the street to the bus stop. "For a minute there, I thought he was going to start dishing out the Nobel Prizes. Imagine the nerve of that guy! As if you or I would stoop low enough to go into politics. Jeez!" His hazel eyes sparkled in the light thrown by the streetlamp.

"Not for you, huh?" Carole asked, that funny feeling growing stronger within her. She was beginning to get an idea.

"Only a fool stands up in front of a crowd to persuade them to do something," Dave assured her. "The wise man, he stays right where he belongs—behind his typewriter. See you in the A.M. Here's my bus."

"Bye." Carole watched Dave climb aboard, and she stood on the corner for a long moment, watching his bus disappear in the direction of Wethersfield Avenue.

I wonder if he's right, she mused, crossing the street to get to her bus stop. He doesn't know everything, after all.

She made a mental note to call Mary Ann after dinner, and only after she was seated in the bus did she think of Steve again. Everything she'd said to Dave about him was true, of course, and he *would* make a good senior class president.

So why did she have this weird feeling that she was going to vote for someone else?

Chapter Three

"Now, MA, it's *extremely* simple. Just repeat after me, 'I place into nomination the name of—'"

"You're a nut, you know that?" Mary Ann said. She was sitting on the floor in Carole's living room, sorting records. The room was becoming littered with album covers as the two girls looked for songs that would be right for Plant Life, the rock group they'd recently organized.

"You were the one who once told me that senior year could be a real bust if you didn't have a direct say in the student government," Carole pointed out, lining up her Stones albums. "You were the one who raised my political consciousness."

"Oh, boy." Mary Ann leaned back on her elbows and stared at the ceiling. "I've created a monster. Listen, I thought that you and I were going to devote all our attention to the band till the end of the term. We were going to practice every afternoon and get gigs around town and design our costumes. All this takes time, Carole. We have to concentrate on toning down Janice's punk-rocker image, and then Ellen's going to take up lots of our time, too—you know what a prima donna she can be. And I have to admit I'm kind of rusty. My keyboard playing leaves a lot to be desired. All this is going to require time and energy. And we still haven't settled on Dave or Stanley for drummer. You'll never have enough time for all this *and* the election."

Carole sighed and gathered up an armful of records. It was four weeks since the afternoon Steve had made his appearance in the newsroom, and she had been watching the approach of nominations with increasing interest. Steve and Sally had thrown themselves into all kinds of elaborate preparations for "The Day," and other kids who'd been sitting on the fence had started to declare themselves as candidates. There was popular Connie Cleveland and also Pete Kelly. They were soon followed by Spike Turner and Melissa Donleavy. Finally, Michael Brooks threw his hat into the ring, and rumor had it that even little Bobby Watson was thinking about running for office.

Well, what are you waiting for? Carole had asked herself glumly each morning when she got up. Didn't *she* have something to offer the senior class? Wasn't she at least as interesting as any of the other candidates? And, she had thought to herself rather smugly, wouldn't Steve be surprised if she ran?

She looked intently at her good friend and hugged the records to her chest. "MA, I've made up my mind. You'd be great as my campaign manager, doing anything that needs doing. Please, I need your help." Her small features were set with determination. "I'll make time for music gigs, too, you'll see," she promised. "Let's get Alice on drums and make it an all-girl band, OK?"

"Yeah, and when are you going to sleep? Only four weeks ago, you told me you didn't have time to go to one little election committee meeting."

"I know," Carole admitted, pulling thoughtfully on her thick braid. "But I've come to a few important decisions since then."

Mary Ann picked up some more records and shoved them into the cabinet. "You're not fooling me for a minute, you know. I'm perfectly clear on what you're up to."

"So, great mastermind, what *am* I up to?" Carole asked smugly.

"Go on! You're still fighting Steve Landy, and you'll do it any way you can."

Carole gave a hoot of laughter. "As my buddy Dave would say, 'Horsefeathers!' " She came over and grabbed Mary Ann by the shoulders. "Say you'll do it, please? You won't be sorry."

"Oh, why am I such a pushover? I know I'm going to regret this."

"No, you won't," Carole cajoled. "Say yes, before I have to twist your arm."

She was on her knees begging when Mrs. Weiss walked in. "You girls rehearsing something for the band?" She frowned at the mess of albums, and Carole and Mary Ann scrambled to their feet, hastily straightening things.

"No, Mom, we were just kidding around."

"I didn't mean to interrupt," Mrs. Weiss said. "I just wanted to warn Mary Ann that if she intends to stay for supper, Mr. Weiss is going to be in a terrible mood. Tax time," she explained.

"Oh, yeah, I know all about that." Mary Ann nodded. "My dad threatened to run away to a desert island last week after he saw his accountant, except my mom told him he didn't know how to forage for nuts and berries, and she'd have to bring him CARE packages every day."

"You're a riot." Carole poked her friend, then swept up the rest of the records with a flourish.

"I was just leaving, actually, Mrs. Weiss," Mary Ann said, smiling politely. "But thanks for asking me to stay."

"OK, dear, but you're welcome to stay if you change your mind." Mrs. Weiss left the room.

"It's really incredible how you do that," Carole

marveled, watching her mother's departing figure.

"Do what?"

"You know what to say to grown-ups all the time. I mean, you can make a silly joke and then turn right around and be as polite as can be."

Mary Ann shrugged. "Politics, that's all. You have to know who to be nice to at the right time. A talent, I might point out, that you don't have."

"I'll learn," Carole assured her in a serious voice. "You know I always do everything I set my mind to." Her dark eyes had a determined gleam.

Mary Ann hesitated a moment and finally reached out and grasped Carole's hand. "If you're really serious about all this, then, of course, I'll do all I can to help."

Carole grinned. "Don't worry, I am."

An excited hum filled the auditorium as the junior class, which consisted of over five hundred students, filed in. Hardly anyone noticed the torrential downpour outside the long windows—they were too concerned with the matter at hand, the nominations for officers of Twain High's senior class.

Each teacher made sure that his or her charges were comfortably settled before taking a seat. When everyone was quiet, Dr. Larkin, the principal of Twain High, began the assembly. He was a large man in his late forties, a former football player, who spoke with a rolling Southern drawl.

Standing up at the podium, he waved for attention. "Aw right now. Y'all know exactly what we're doin' here, and I don't want to take up too much of anyone's time," he said, his words filling the large hall.

"Then get on with it, please," Dave whispered to Carole. She was clutching her hands tightly together, and every once in a while, she would wipe them on her purple corduroy skirt. She couldn't remember the last time she'd worn a skirt to school.

"We are gathered here," Dr. Larkin continued, "to select the officers of next year's senior class. These positions are not to be taken lightly. Holding an office is like holding yourself up to public scrutiny. Some of us ought to think twice before we stand up and make speeches."

There was a rustle of laughter, followed by stern looks from some of the teachers. Dave had closed his eyes and slumped down in his seat, pulling the visor of his baseball cap down as a shade. Mary Ann, seated directly in back of Carole, was alternately coughing and clearing her throat. Carole could see Steve on the other side of the auditorium. He was sitting up straight in his seat and seemed to be hanging on to every word Dr. Larkin uttered. And there was Sally Scott, craning her neck around periodically to look at the people sitting farthest away from her, as if she was trying to determine who would be for and who against her.

"I suppose y'all have heard enough from me today," Dr. Larkin said, looking around the room. "And, therefore, it is with great pleasure that I turn over the microphone to the moderator of today's assembly, current senior class president, Mr. John Haynes."

A smattering of applause greeted John Haynes's approach to the podium. Carole had never liked him much. She thought he was really egotistical. But Carole did have to admit that he wasn't a bad president. His arrogance never stood in the way of his getting things done for the school.

"Hi, everybody," John began, flashing a pearly smile around the large hall. "Now this could be one of the saddest days of my life, but"— he threw up his hands resignedly—"it's all in the cards, you know. We grow up, graduate, and go on to bigger and better things. I'm going to pass on the mantle of the presidency of the senior class with great reluctance, but with understanding and, I hope, respect for the person who comes after me."

"Oh, buddy, will you can it already!" Dave muttered so loudly that everyone from the third row back could hear. A couple of kids snickered.

"I'll just run down the specifics now, if I may," Haynes continued. "As you know, this is just a preliminary. In order to qualify as a bona fide candidate, each nominee must have fifty signatures on a formal petition. Each nominee must go before the elections committee and pass muster. And finally, each nominee has to go out there and campaign his brains out!"

Dave slipped further down in his seat. "You never had any brains to start with, doofus."

"Shut up, Dave," Carole hissed. Now she was starting to get nervous.

"Nominations are now in order," John said. "The election will be May seventh. As you know, the candidate who gets the most votes on that day will be president, second highest will be vice-president, third highest will be secretary, and fourth will be treasurer." He looked around the room, slowly scanning the hands raised in the air. "OK, we can start. Yes?" He pointed at one of the hands.

"I place into nomination for president of the senior class, Steve Landy."

Carole looked over to see Max Schoen pop back down in his seat. He and Steve were really good friends.

"Second," yelled Ron Yang.

John wrote down Steve's name and then pointed to the next nominator, Eleanor Laiken. "Y—yes?"

"I nominate Sally Scott for president," Eleanor said primly.

"Second," called wimpy Irv Bates.

Carole turned to glare at Mary Ann, who had a tight, pinched look on her otherwise pretty face. Her cheeks were about as red as her hair.

"OK, OK," she muttered, sticking her hand halfway up. Then they heard Jack Dunn nominate his best friend, Pete Kelly, who was head of the junior class finance committee. A reluctant second came only after John had asked for it several times. Pete Kelly was a real whiz when it came to math, but he could barely carry on a coherent conversation. The word that came out of his mouth most often was "huh."

There were five more nominations. The first of these was for Melissa Donleavy, and the second for Spike Turner. He was a big star on the football team. Someone nominated Bobby Watson, secretary of the junior class, and there was a ripple of approval when the second came. Then Michael Brooks was nominated. His father was a representative of the Connecticut state legislature, so running for office was probably in his blood. The next nomination was for Connie Cleveland, the most popular girl in school. Then the large room became very quiet.

"Any further nominations?" asked John.

Silence. Carole did not turn around again, but she was staring daggers, backward of course, at Mary Ann.

At last she heard, "Uh, yeah, I have one."

"Yes?" John was waiting along with everyone else. Finally Mary Ann blurted out, "I place into nomination for the position of senior class president, Carole Weiss."

"*Are you out of your mind, idiot!*" shrieked Dave, jumping from his seat in a panic.

"I second the motion." It was Ellen Heym, the lead singer of Plant Life.

When she heard it out loud, Carole felt more scared than she'd ever been in her life. Why had she come up with this dumb idea in the first place? What did she know about being president of anything? And the fact that everyone was acting like it was awful made it even more awful. At this particular moment, she wondered whether she really wanted the job. But that was the least of her worries now. If she didn't get fifty signatures on her petition, she wouldn't even be in the running. And then she'd be truly embarrassed. She'd have to go cringing around school for the rest of the semester. Not to mention listening to Dave's dumb gibes.

Maybe she would withdraw her own nomination. She could say it was a terrible mistake and that Mary Ann had only spoken up because she was her best friend and happened to be out of her mind. But it was too late. John Haynes thumped his hand on the lectern and declared that nominations were closed. Carole felt a wave of fear wash over her. She knew she was going to have to make a speech, and she knew what she wanted to say, but the very idea of doing it now filled her with terror.

"Could the nominees please approach the stage?" John asked.

"Don't you go up there!" Dave spat in her ear when she rose tentatively from her seat. "Nobody in this room's going to make you president, sister. Believe me!"

Carole whirled on him, her eyes narrowing, her mind suddenly changed by that one comment—a comment that bore a great resemblance to Steve's over a year before about women presidents. "That's what you think, pal," she answered back. Head held high, shoulders squared, she marched bravely to the stage of Twain High's auditorium.

Sally, Melissa, Pete, Spike, Michael, Bobby, and Connie were already standing around at the foot of the steps, but Steve waited until Carole was nearly up to his place before he started walking. She had no choice but to march along beside him, but she didn't look at him. She knew exactly what she'd see if she looked into his eyes. An infuriating, condescending smile that would show her how ridiculous he thought it was for her to be running for school office. Carole kept walking.

Dr. Larkin, beaming down at the assembly, got up to shake hands with each candidate. He drew them together in a semicircle at the front of the stage and presented them to the rest of the students.

"Here they are, everybody," Dr. Larkin announced. "I know that they all wish to serve the senior class and Twain High to the best of their ability. Now, it's up to you."

Carole hung back, reluctant to get anywhere near that threatening microphone. It looked like a huge silver bullet aimed right at her heart. Why couldn't she remember any of the campaign promises she'd come up with? Dave's words rang in her head, blotting out everything else: "There's no fool like a young fool."

Steve took his prepared notes from his pocket, went to his place center stage, and spoke loudly and distinctly, his deep voice booming through the mike, up to the rafters of the auditorium. "Once again, I'd like to thank my supporters," he began—too humbly, Carole thought—"and to assure them that I will work through faculty and student channels to achieve the goals we've all set for ourselves. Senior year, as we all know, brings with it the biggest rewards and the most difficult trials of our entire high-school career, and it's up to you to select officers who will represent you best. I want you to know that I've worked hard as debating team president, but that's nothing in comparison to what I'll do next year, if I'm elected to the highest office of the senior class."

Carole glared at him as a ripple of enthusiastic approval spread through the audience. So what was he doing this year? Holding back? Why was he being so general? Didn't he have any specific platform and particular reforms he wanted to push through? Come to think of it, what was wrong with the ones she'd thought up herself? Maybe she wouldn't be such a wimpy candidate after all.

And Steve's speech was so like him—so noble and self-righteous—but what did he mean? It reminded her of that old saw: Every day in every way, I'm getting better and better.

Horsefeathers!

Why should Steve do any more for the school as a senior than he had as a junior? Carole didn't want to blow a lot of hot air around. She wanted to discuss real issues, things that could actually be accomplished with work.

The second speaker was Spike Turner. Spike told a lot of jokes that weren't very funny and then made way for Melissa, who recounted everything she had done for the junior class. After she named each extracurricular activity, she apologized for not having done more. It was a terrible speech, Carole thought, and the bored faces in the first few rows were testimony to Melissa's lack of political finesse. Then Connie spoke, and she was a real hit. There was something so likable about her that the content of her speech was sort of lost in the general aura of her peppy personality.

Sally Scott was next. She withdrew a prepared speech from the pocket of her plaid skirt and cleared her throat. She smoothed her bangs and looked around the large hall, trying to take in each face. Evidently she'd done her homework. Carole begrudgingly acknowledged that Sally knew what she was doing.

"Dr. Larkin, faculty of Twain High, fellow students, and fellow nominees," she began. "I would like to thank you from the bottom of my heart for this vote of confidence and to tell you right off, without mincing words, what I intend to do for you if elected president of the senior class.

"As you know, senior year events can get very expensive, and I'm aware of the difficulties involved in meeting these costs."

Carole made a face. Sally Scott's father was loaded! What did she care about expenses?

"The senior prom, for one. I intend to work diligently and tirelessly to lower the bid for each couple at least twenty dollars from this year's bid. I believe this can be arranged through higher attendance, careful management of food and entertainment, and possible use of as yet uncommitted booster committee funds."

Her last words were drowned out by a cheer of approval from the juniors. Carole stared at the floor, thinking that, in fact, this was a marvelous idea. *Phooey.*

"The next item on the agenda will be the senior yearbook. The yearbook committee will be working their heads off to provide us with the finest product of any class so far. The photography, the layout, the writing, the advertising, will all require a lot of money, and I believe that I can lower the price of the book by some cleverly planned functions—faculty-student softball games, pay parking in the school lot for lower classmen, perhaps a raffle. The possibilities are endless! Twain High simply needs an effective leader to see these projects through. If you elect me senior class president, I promise to deliver." She ended her speech by smacking one fist into her palm. The response of the audience was deafening.

Carole felt like crawling under the lectern and staying there. Why hadn't she written her speech down, or at least prepared some notes? Her only consolation was that Sally had gotten a bigger hand than Steve. She sneaked a look at him out of the corner of her eye but was disappointed to see that he appeared undisturbed by Sally's popularity. Always the politician, he was not going to show by word or deed or look that he was behind.

Pete Kelly shuffled up to the podium and glanced shyly at the assembled group. "Um, thanks for the nomination. I hope you'll vote for me, and. . . ." He searched the air for a punchy end to his sentence. Then his broad face lit up as the answer came to him. It was as if he'd just seen the answer to an algebra problem written out in skywriting above him.

"I'd like you all to know," he finished, "that my calculator will keep on pumping. Thank you." With a funny little nod, he stepped away from the podium, and everyone applauded politely.

Next came Michael, whose polished speech made Carole suspect that his father had been giving him lessons. After him, Bobby Watson said a few brief words that were very much to the point. He was a stutterer, and Carole admired him for having the guts to get up and speak in front of such a large group.

Now it was her turn. Carole waited for silence and tried to calm her shaking, sweaty hands by gripping the lectern like a life preserver. Her mouth was dry, and she couldn't get her breath. She tried to picture herself playing with her rock band when the rhythms were flowing. Then, there wasn't a speck of nervousness in her whole body. Performing was *nothing* compared to making a speech. That was good fun, whereas this was like talking in class when you hadn't read the assignment. Every impulse from her brain to her nervous system told her to run. But she couldn't back down now. She adjusted the mike down to her level.

"It's really great to be up here," she lied blatantly. "And I want to thank you all, faculty and students both, for giving me a chance to prove that I have something to contribute."

Her voice sounded a little too high and tense to her ears. She fought to control it. "Some of you may know that up till now, my main interest has been the music club. But I suppose part of life is change, and the best part of going to a school like Twain High is having the opportunity to move on from one set of activities to another where you feel you can be of greater use to your fellow students."

She could just imagine Dave's reaction. At this very minute, she was certain he was sitting in the back of the auditorium mumbling a put-down, while she was trying her utmost to sound convincing.

"Now we come down to the crunch," she said, leaning forward just as she had seen real politicians do on television debates. "What can I offer? What will I do for you if I'm elected?"

Good question, Weiss. Oh, will you please speak clearly and not pause so much! She could feel Steve's eyes on her.

"The senior year of high school is traditionally a time of increased responsibility and privilege. It's not all proms and yearbooks, you know. Those are just isolated events at the end of the long haul. Being a senior is preparation for everything that comes afterward, and it ought to give us all time to reflect and think about our place in the big scheme of things. We ought to help out in the community." She looked around to see if she was getting her point across, but nobody seemed to care very much about helping out in the community.

"Not just that," she continued. "Being a senior also ought to carry with it its own special stuff because after all"—she looked around and winked, fighting for casualness—" 'You've come a long way, baby.' "

Her first laugh. It sounded warm and cozy, like a roaring fire on a winter's night. Whoever the appreciative laughers were out there, she loved them.

"And, therefore, I am proposing the establishment of a senior lounge, a room in the school that will be ours alone, and where coffee and Coke will flow freely. If I am elected, one of my first duties will be to arrange the setup and maintenance of this room for the greater glory of our senior class!"

A cheer burst the air. Carole stood clutching the lectern, dumbfounded at the reaction to this idea, which had just come to her the night before, as she was about to fall asleep. Well, it *was* a pretty good idea, when she thought about it a little. But was it enough of a platform to guarantee election to the presidency? And could she even get permission to do it? She glanced over at Dr. Larkin, who was smiling his usual noncommittal smile.

Carole cleared her throat and raised her hands for silence. Now, she needed a windup. "Naturally," she began, "this is only a very small part of my campaign pledge to you. As a fellow Twain High student, I want you to know that I think the presidency—and the other offices, for that matter—should be a cooperative deal. Only by tapping the excellent ideas and strong feelings of my constituency would I be properly able to govern. I wouldn't stand up in front of you and make speeches the way I am now"—she threw in a smile, something that gained her another ripple of laughter—"but I'd leave decisions mostly in your hands and simply be the arbitrator. Senior year is serious business," she concluded, "so we all have to be president together."

Then she nodded to the crowd. She was thrilled to hear warm applause following her speech. She backed away from the podium, smiling and waving. She really felt good. Here she had been doubting that her abilities were anywhere near as good as the others, and she seemed to have made the biggest impression of all. She took another step backward and then suddenly she caught her heel on one of the microphone outlets. She tripped and, unable to stop her fall, twisted and went down like a stone and lay sprawled on the stage. It was the most humiliating thing that had ever happened in her entire life!

Covering her face with her hands, she rolled over and sat up. Oh, this was horrible! Now everyone was laughing at her, not with her. Their clapping was mixed with guffaws and chortles. Carole wanted to drop through the floor. She'd blown the whole thing.

Then she felt a hand on her arm. "Here, let me help." Steve's teasing brown eyes gazed down at her, and he reached for her, executing a smooth dip as he swept her up onto her feet. Those lousy kids were *still* laughing!

Carole jerked away, releasing herself from Steve's grip. "Thank you, but I'm perfectly all right," she spat at him, walking away stiffly. There was nothing in the world as terrible as this. The other candidates had filed offstage ahead of her, and as she marched up the long aisle to take her place with her homeroom class, she knew that every single eye in the place was glued on her. Oh, she wanted to die!

Dr. Larkin was making another speech, but she didn't hear a word. She took her place next to Dave and could actually feel the heat radiating from her burning cheeks. Mary Ann patted her sympathetically on the shoulder, but she didn't acknowledge her friend's touch.

After what seemed to Carole like another hundred years or so, the assembly ended, and everyone filed out of the auditorium. Carole's next period was lunch, but she didn't feel at all hungry.

"Well," Dave said, chuckling, when they were out in the corridor, "you sure made a spectacle of yourself. In more ways than one." Then he just walked away.

Carole couldn't remember ever feeling so alone.

Chapter Four

Carole wandered down to the newsroom after her last class, not even thinking about the consequences of making an appearance there now that she was a nominee.

When she walked through the door, about five reporters jumped her, a lot of eager-beaver Dan Rathers and Walter Cronkites.

"Where's the senior lounge going to be, Carole?"

"How can you beat out Miss Popularity—I mean, Connie?"

"How many names do you have on your petition so far?"

"What makes you think you'll be a better president than Landy or Brooks or Scott?" She was barraged with one insistent question after another. The reporters were like a bunch of hungry ants, swarming over an abandoned picnic.

"Aw, guys, gimme a break," she muttered,

but then she saw Dave staring reproachfully at her from his desk across the room. His look clearly stated that she wasn't entitled to any breaks now that she was a candidate. Now she was fair game.

"OK, one at a time, please," she said, bravely stationing herself in the middle of the crazed herd.

"What about the lounge, Carole?"

"Well," she said, thinking fast, "there's that rehearsal room on the top floor. Since the drama club revamped their little theater, nobody uses that space, and it's a big room. Also it's isolated from the clubs and classrooms. It's possible we could get some parent to donate a coffee machine, and then we'd just set up a senior fund for eats and decorating." As she spoke, the plan became a bit more feasible.

"Tell us more about your platform, Carole."

"How're you gonna beat out Landy?"

"Say." Dave pushed aside the most annoying of the reporters. "You probably can get most of that info from Ms. Weiss's campaign manager." He took Carole by one wrist and led her away. "I want to talk to you," he said, grabbing his books.

They escaped with relatively little hassle into the basement hallway, at which point Dave turned on her. "This is a joke, right? April Fools'?"

"No joke, Dave. I'm doing it. I'm even going to win—maybe."

"Ha!"

"But you've got to help me. You're the one who's always telling me I don't have any political savvy." She ran her hands nervously through her dark hair. "That was practically off the top of my head—what I said up there this morning. I don't know how to run a campaign."

"Tough, kid." He shrugged. "You should have thought long and hard about that before. Now it's all in your lap."

"Some friend!" she grumbled, planting her hands on her hips. "I expected you to back me, not turn on me."

"Yeah?" he said angrily, sticking his face right near hers. "And what'd you just do to me? I lost my good buddy—who turns out to be a snake in the grass."

"What are you—?"

"And who doesn't even let me audition for drummer of her rock group, but that's another story," he continued.

"It's an all-girl band, Dave, for heaven's sake!" They were both practically shouting now. "Why all this heavy punishment?" she asked in desperation. "What'd I do to you?"

"C'mon, Carole, don't play dumb. How many times have we knocked those kids who play school games? Huh? How many editorials of mine have you read that went along with the crowd?" His eyes burned with rage and disappointment. She had betrayed him.

Carole sighed. "I guess you weren't even listening to me this morning. The reason I went into the idiotic performing seal act in the first place, Dave, was to do it differently. I don't think the Connie Clevelands and Steve Landys of this world ought to run it—I think people like *us* should!"

"US!" He snorted. "You're too much." He turned away from her.

"Dave, I have some real things I want to do, not just fluff. Look, how about that elementary school lunch program you wrote the editorial about? Maybe I can get the kids to do something constructive for a change. How about organizing senior trips to nursing homes for volunteer work, or to Washington to lobby for students' rights?"

"I don't know—it doesn't concern me," Dave scoffed.

"You could run for office, too, you know. Your height isn't stopping you this time," she added, throwing a handful of salt on the wound.

"You know so much, right? Well, you can take your campaign and do whatever you want with it. I'll never cop out!" He stalked away down the hall and disappeared past the exit sign, leaving Carole standing there with her mouth open.

Now that Dave had refused to help her, Carole felt *really* lost. She knew that campaigning wasn't his style, but she had figured that out of friendship he'd give her some advice and support. With that hope shattered, she didn't know what to do. She just wanted to go home, lock herself up with her rock group, and play her brains out. Politics was not her thing, and now in one short day, she'd dived in way over her head. It wasn't just having a lot of brainy ideas—it was somehow getting them through to others. And getting them done.

She felt like a real criminal sneaking out of school, but she knew that at any moment another reporter might pop up and quiz her, or some classmate might walk up and swear he was voting for Steve, just to spite her.

Steve! She shook her head, filled with terrible fears about going through with the campaign. If Steve beat her, he would be insufferable their senior year. She'd seen that look on his face when he'd helped her up onstage. He obviously thought she was running just to make it tougher for him. Well, that wasn't true—despite what MA and Dave said.

But suppose she beat him? The thought was startling, but it brought a surprised smile to her face. Well, why not? Her candidacy was going to be different from everyone else's. She just might possibly—what was that expression they always used?—capture the imagination of the public.

Then there was another possibility. Maybe, because she was inexperienced, she wouldn't get enough votes to be president, but she'd come in second or third and get some other office, less responsible, but no less meaningful. That wouldn't be so bad either.

Another thought suddenly occurred to Carole. What if she and Steve *both* got posts? It was a real possibility, considering the fact that there were four positions available. If that happened, she'd have to spend a lot of time with him next year—they'd *have* to learn to cooperate. Although that idea would have seemed altogether unthinkable to Carole just a few days before, anything seemed possible now. As long as hers was the higher position, she knew she could deal with Steve easily. Not that she felt competitive with him; of course not. It was just that she wouldn't be able to stand Steve's condescending attitude if she had to be his subordinate next year. With this new incentive in mind—to have the power to veto Steve's suggestions whenever she felt like it—Carole renewed her determination. As she walked slowly to the bus stop, her smile disappeared, and her expression became grim. This was war, and she was readier than ever to throw herself right into the thick of battle.

Her mother was sorting groceries when she got home, and without being asked, Carole pitched in. Her mother gave her a funny look but then decided to leave well enough alone. It wasn't often that her daughter did chores willingly. Carole wasn't lazy or a shirker; it was simply, as she so often explained to her parents, that life was very short, and she had a lot of more important things to get done.

"Have a good day, dear?" Mrs. Weiss asked as Carole stacked cans of vegetables in the cupboard.

"Um." Carole went back for another armload.

"Anything going on with the music club?"

"Nope." Carole's thoughts were totally focused on the election. She simply couldn't bother thinking up answers to her mom's questions.

"Well, what's new?" Carole's father asked, walking in and closing the kitchen door behind him. He looked very cheery, Carole thought, probably because his insurance business was booming.

"Hi, dear." Mrs. Weiss went over to give her husband a kiss and then returned to the kitchen table, where she was beginning dinner preparations.

"How's my girl?" Mr. Weiss came up behind Carole and tickled the back of her neck. She shrugged his hand away and gave an embarrassed laugh.

"Hi, Dad."

"Well, well, everybody looks busy in here, now

don't they?" He removed his hat and coat and started toward the living room. "Guess I'll leave my girls to their work." He sighed contentedly and strolled out of the room.

Carole bristled at his comment. If there was anything she hated, it was a patronizing male attitude about "women's work." Her father had just reminded her of all the disagreements she and Steve used to have.

"Gotta get to my homework, Mom," she said hastily. "See you later."

"Carole!" Mrs. Weiss frowned at her daughter.

"What?"

"I thought you were going to help out with dinner tonight. What's going on with you lately?"

"Huh? What do you mean?" Carole asked suspiciously.

"You seem so preoccupied, I don't know. . . . Anything you'd like to talk about?"

"Um, well. . . ." Carole weighed the options. She was going to have to tell her parents she was running for senior class president some time or other. She wasn't sure what the reaction would be, and she had to present the information under the best possible circumstances. If she told her mother now, before she had her campaign completely mapped out, it would come out all wrong. Her confusion could jinx the whole thing.

She shrugged. "Not really. I just feel a little

tired, and I'm worried about all this homework I have to do. Would it be OK if I helped you tomorrow night instead?"

"Well . . . I guess it would be all right," her mother said.

"Thanks, Mom." Carole made a quick exit out of the kitchen, ignoring her mother's concerned expression.

She knew she was being obnoxious, but there was really nothing she could do about it. She just wasn't the type of person who could convincingly pull off an act. Some politician she was going to make! In the meantime, her parents were going to think there was something seriously wrong if she didn't snap out of it soon.

She looked at her algebra assignment but gave up without trying to do a single problem. If only Dave were on her side, but now he was thoroughly disgusted with her. There was MA, who'd been reluctantly corralled into this brilliant scheme, but what did she know? Less than Carole, probably. MA had only agreed to be her campaign manager because she was a good friend. All MA really wanted to do was to get going with Plant Life, and any other activities would only take time away from the rock group.

Well, what could I do all by myself? Carole decided she had to start thinking constructively. She'd get some books and read about campaigns past and present. She'd perfect her image and speaking techniques. She'd go door to door all over Hartford to get signatures for her petition.

Would kids sign if they knew she was the serious, issue-oriented candidate? They might just be bored to tears by her constructive plans and programs.

Then there was the problem of her senior lounge brainstorm. She had no idea how she'd ever make that happen, but she would worry about that later on. *Much* later on.

The phone rang once, and someone picked it up downstairs in the kitchen. Then Carole heard footsteps on the stairs, and in a second there was a soft knock at her door.

"Yes?"

Her mother opened the door. "Dear, it's for you," she said, in the oddest voice. "It's . . . it's Steve Landy."

Carole exhaled sharply and dropped her head into her hands. She should have known he'd call to gloat. What could she say to him?

"OK, Mom." Slowly, she pushed back her hair and looked up at her mother, who was wearing this funny little Cheshire cat grin. Carole didn't say a word but sat there stolidly at her desk, not even moving a finger toward the night table beside her bed where her extension phone was. Her mother sighed and gently closed the door again.

Carole walked over to the phone and frowned at it. Then she took the receiver gingerly in one hand and put it to her ear, flipping her hair over her other shoulder. She waited until she heard her mother hang up the phone downstairs. Then, as casually as she could, she said, "Hi, Steve."

"Hey, hello!"

The sound of his voice on the phone brought back past memories in a rush. When they were going together, they used to talk every night after dinner, no matter how much time they'd spent together that day. Carole would kick off her shoes, tuck her feet under her, and settle in for a good, long conversation. As she recalled, they'd had few arguments when they talked on the phone—probably because she couldn't be provoked by his laughing, teasing eyes.

"What's up?" she asked. Let him say what he called to say, she thought stubbornly. I'm not giving him any chances to walk all over me.

"Well, you sure surprised me today," he said, laughing. "By the way, are you OK? That was quite a tumble you took."

"I'm fine, thanks," she responded curtly. He *would* bring up the moment of her greatest humiliation!

"Say, whatever got you on the campaign trail?" he asked. "I'm really curious."

"The old school spirit, I suppose," she told him. "Actually, I was tired of the way things were being run. I figured I could do better." For some reason she couldn't resist the dig. It reminded her of the way they used to be together, scrapping and fighting all the time.

"What's wrong with me for president?" he asked, without a trace of grumpiness in his voice. "Or Sally Scott, for that matter?"

"Old blood," Carole said decisively, making up her mind even as she spoke. "You guys have had a monopoly on school affairs long enough. I think it's time some of the rest of us got involved."

"Hmmm, you may have a point," Steve said graciously.

She frowned down at the telephone. "You don't mean that. You think it's really dumb of me to run."

"No, I don't. That's why I called, Carole. I want to wish you all the luck in the world."

Why is he being so nice? she wondered. Or was this what politicians did before they started fighting tooth and nail to beat out their opponents?

"Thanks. Same to you," she responded, figuring she had to be at least as generous as he was.

"I just thought you ought to know your senior lounge idea was fantastic—right on target."

"Oh, it was something I'd been working on for a while," she said glibly.

"But—now I hope you take this in the right spirit—your acceptance speech was a little ragged."

She felt that old battling impulse bounce right back into place. "Oh, really?"

"Yeah, well, that's perfectly understandable. You've never gotten up in public before." He sounded so condescending! Carole was instantly livid.

"I guess I'll just have to scrape by on my measly capabilities, then," she muttered between clenched teeth. "Nice of you to call, Steve. Bye."

Before she could slam down the receiver, he yelled in her ear, "Hey! Come back here! Carole, please don't get mad. I only meant maybe you could use a few pointers on technique, that's all."

"Sure," she agreed. "And I assume you're going to coach me?"

"Well, why not?"

She shifted in her seat uncomfortably. "That's kind of like the rabbit letting the fox teach him escape routes, isn't it?"

"Carole." Steve laughed. "I'm not out to sabotage you, if that's what you mean. This is a genuine offer of help."

"You mean no matter how many pointers you give me, you'll still win, right?"

He chuckled his self-confident chuckle. "That's about it."

"Fat chance, Landy!" she cut in hotly. "Wouldn't you be surprised if I triumphed all by myself."

He was silent for a moment, and then he said, "I'd be real surprised. As a matter of fact, I'd be dumbfounded. But I wouldn't stand in your way, Carole. If this is what you really want—if it's something you've been hoping and planning for, for months—I'll be glad for you."

She was immediately brought up short by her own reasons for going into the election. No, of course this wasn't her goal in life, but she did love a challenge, and this was one thing she hadn't tackled yet. She knew she could offer something that no other candidate could, just because she was high-principled Carole Weiss, who always did things a bit differently from everybody else. But from the earnest tone of his voice, she knew perfectly well that being senior class president had been Steve's goal since the first day of freshman term. Why should she casually go after something that was so very important to others? For the first time since her decision to run, Carole thought about the other candidates' feelings.

Softening, she sighed into the telephone. "Well, it sure will be weird, won't it, if we tie for first place."

"You think that's a possibility?" he asked.

"I don't know. Maybe. Or maybe neither of us will win."

Carole didn't mention her new hope that they would each be elected and that she would hold the higher post.

"Let's get together and talk about it," he suggested at once.

"What? Oh, I didn't mean. . . ." She laughed nervously. "Have to keep the old fighting energy up, don't we?"

"Do we?" His question was so warm, and he so clearly wanted to make up for past wrongs, Carole almost melted. This phone call wasn't just a political move. And she couldn't doubt his good wishes for her. But going out with him would defeat the whole purpose of running against him—she knew that for a fact. If she started really liking Steve again and feeling all warm and tingly whenever he smiled at her or touched her hand, she'd pay less attention to her campaign. Her cutting edge would be dulled, and she'd have no fight left in her. Still, she felt a little guilty for wanting to beat him in this election. But much as she was tempted to just have a friendly conversation with him, she realized it would be a mistake. She hated to admit it, but MA was right. She hadn't forgotten Steve.

"Steve, my mom's calling me. It's dinner now or never. Say, thanks for the call. I really mean that."

"Think about my offer," he insisted, not at all upset by her delaying tactic. "It would really make the campaign a lot more interesting. More exciting for everyone, if you get my point."

She knew what was behind his words, and she willed herself not to be influenced by him. It would not do her the least bit of good to fall for him all over again. Especially not now.

"Bye, Steve. See you tomorrow."

"Good. I'll look for you tomorrow." His tone was challenging. Then he hung up. Carole stood looking at the phone for a few minutes and had to wrench herself away from her thoughts when her mother finally did call her for dinner. If she'd had a lot on her mind before the phone call, now she was overflowing. The chore of sitting and having a conversation with her parents while she ate seemed particularly awful.

"How's Steve?" Her mother grinned as she passed the bowl of mashed potatoes.

"Fine." Carole took a spoonful before passing it to her father.

"What's new with him?" asked Mr. Weiss.

If only her father would quit asking what was new. It would be impossible to dream up enough answers to that question, even if she were in the mood, considering how many times her father asked it each week. Well, she might as well tell all.

"He's running for senior class president. Nominations were today."

"That's nice for him. I suppose it's logical he'll win, since he's so active in school affairs, right?" her mother asked cheerily. She was clearly waiting for Carole to get to the good part—the romantic angle.

"I don't know." Carole took a bite of fish and chewed it thoughtfully. "He's got some pretty stiff competition. Sally Scott is his biggest threat, but there's also Melissa Donleavy, Connie Cleveland, Michael Brooks, Bobby Watson, Spike Turner, and Pete Kelly. And me," she added, digging into her potatoes.

"You!" her father yelled.

"Carole, you're kidding!" Her mother's fork clattered onto her plate.

"Well, don't everyone congratulate me at once," said their red-faced daughter.

"Oh, darling, don't take it the wrong way." Her mother reached over to pat her hand, which was clenching and releasing her paper napkin. "It's just that you've never been very school-spirited. Why, I remember even in sixth grade, when everyone else was lining up to get picked as crossing guards, so they could wear those neat badges, you said it was dumb."

Her father nodded his agreement. "Definitely against anything establishment, even in those days. Sweetheart, we love you—you know that—but it's so unlike you."

"I really don't care what either of you think." Carole's voice was all quavery, and she was scared that she was going to burst into tears right at the table. "I'm going to win this election—you'll see."

"But, dear, what about Steve?" Mrs. Weiss asked in a worried tone.

"What about him?"

"It's just . . . well, it seems sort of hopeless to run against the school favorite, doesn't it? Are you sure you're not just doing this to prove something to him?"

Mr. Weiss nodded. "And he's such a nice boy."

Carole stared with open hostility at her parents, who were lined up against her. How could they support Steve Landy over their own daughter! Well, naturally, the reason was obvious. He was a fake grown-up, doing everything in perfect imitation of his elders, while she, the silly little daughter, was good for nothing but rock groups and other teen activities. How could she, Carole Weiss, be their child? It seemed much more likely that they had found her under a guitar case somewhere and had taken her home out of pity.

"If you'll excuse me," she said evenly, "I'm finished with dinner. I have to go call Mary Ann and start planning my election strategies. She's my campaign manager," she added, on her way out.

And then, just to make things worse than they already were, both her parents roared with laughter at the same time. Carole slammed the dining-room door with every ounce of energy left in her. What did *they* know, anyway?

Chapter Five

"I'm not going to give up!" Carole's small face was furrowed with intensity. She hadn't slept very well the previous night, but she was speeding around on all cylinders despite her lack of rest.

"I never said you should," Mary Ann assured her. She slurped the rest of her container of milk through her straw and put it on her tray beside the remains of her lunch. The cafeteria was pretty empty, since it was the first beautiful spring day, and most people were outside, taking advantage of lunch period before they had to go back to their classrooms again.

"You think I'm an imbecile," Carole said fretfully. "You and everyone else, but it doesn't matter. I'll stand alone."

"Oh, don't feel so sorry for yourself," Mary Ann said. "You'll never win this thing without my invaluable help."

Carole was about to protest, but when she looked into her friend's face, she knew she was right. "What do I do first?" she asked earnestly.

"OK!" Mary Ann banged a determined fist on the lunchroom table. "The petition, first of all. You need fifty—count 'em—fifty names, none of them forged. Now, you can't just corner people in the halls after class. People are always rushing off to get someplace, so that strategy will only work for Sally or Steve or Michael—candidates, who don't need much image building."

"Much what?" Carole felt as though she were in over her head.

"Image building. You've seen it on TV, how candidates run around to shopping centers shaking hands and kissing babies."

Carole frowned and shook her head. "I don't think I'm going to like what you're about to suggest."

"Sure!" Mary Ann pushed her tray aside and moved over closer to Carole. "You ring doorbells right before dinner and give the kids your speech when they come to the door. You go to the mall Saturday afternoon and make the rounds. Most of our gang is window-shopping at Fashion Alley, so that's easy. You cover the record store, of course, the video arcade, and Burger King. There are so many possibilities, Carole."

Carole moaned. "Oh, boy. So I get my fifty names by acting like a clown around town. Then what?"

"Then you pour on the steam. The candidates always give their platform speech about a week before the election, right? You've got to be right on top of all the issues. I think, with your writing skills and everything, you should just get Dave to let you publish a piece about yourself and your candidacy in the *Herald*."

Carole shook her head. "He's so friendly to me right now, he'd probably print my piece in invisible ink."

"Very funny." Mary Ann scratched her head, thinking furiously. "Now as far as I can tell, you have a tight constituency already, albeit small, people who will definitely vote for you. All you have to do is expand your horizons." Mary Ann went over to put her tray on the conveyer belt and made room for Carole to do the same.

"Yeah?" she asked curiously. "Who's my constituency?"

"Well, there's the band. Ellen seconded you, remember? And kids in the music club. And probably some people on the paper." She was trying to be kind, but she didn't have much to back up her case.

"A big fat total of fifteen at the very most. Need I remind you, MA, that there are over five hundred kids in our class who will be voting?"

"Hmmm. Not a terrific percentage," MA calculated. "But we're getting there."

Carole shook her head and said nothing. It really did seem hopeless.

"Guess who called me last night?" she ventured as they walked back into the corridor.

"Who?"

"Steve. He offered to help out with my campaign." She looked at her friend expectantly.

"Oh? Why would he want to do a thing like that?"

"I don't know." Carole bit her lip. "He's a nice guy?"

"Wrong." Mary Ann shook her head emphatically. "Look, I don't think he'd do anything to hurt you, but maybe he'd get you into a corner and tell you everything you're messing up, until you felt so bad about your chances, you'd just give up."

"That doesn't sound like Steve," Carole protested.

Mary Ann shrugged. "Maybe not. You know him better than I do. But keep in mind," she went on, waggling a finger in Carole's face, "all's fair in love and war. Oh, Ellen called me last night. She's totally bananas about getting Plant Life off the ground. The ninny, she thinks we're going to have paying gigs by the beginning of the summer."

"Oh?" Carole was only half-listening. She was still thinking about Steve.

"Yeah. Her aunt is head of her church's bazaar committee. She's getting us booked to play a set there, and the date's May ninth."

Carole grabbed her arm and whirled her

around. "But the election is May seventh. How am I supposed to make time before then for rehearsal?"

Mary Ann shrugged. "Hey, you should have thought of that before you got me to nominate you for this ridiculous job, Carole. You committed yourself to the group first."

"I know, but—"

"We've got a rehearsal Sunday at four, Janice's basement. Don't be late," she called as the bell rang and she dashed away from Carole down the corridor. Carole stood there, staring after her, a sinking feeling in the pit of her stomach.

She was out the front door of Twain High only minutes after the last bell of the day rang. The fresh air was cool, easing her confused brain, and she walked quickly to get out of range before kids began pouring into the yard.

The first place she had to go was to the public library, a healthy walk that would give her time to think. When she got there, she located copies of *Robert's Rules of Order*, *How to Be an Effective Speaker*, and *Improving Your Powers of Persuasion*. These were her required reading, and she would memorize them if she had to.

She circled the park and started back toward the center of downtown Hartford. High Street was crowded with shoppers and businessmen playing hooky from work to enjoy the beautiful weather. She turned onto Ann Street and hesitated only a moment before entering a store called The Optical Illusion.

Carole had never worn glasses, but she'd always loved coming in here with her mother when she got new frames. Carole always tried on a few herself, just for the effect. She hadn't been in this store for at least three years, and she hoped that nobody would recognize her. The great thing about the place was that they had little booths with video machines so that you could see yourself in your new glasses. Perfect!

"Hello, may I help you, young lady?" A middle-aged man in a shiny blue suit wearing heavy horn-rimmed spectacles smiled down at her.

"Uh, just looking, thanks." She scanned the shelves hastily, trying to screw up her courage.

"New prescription? Or just want some new frames?" The pesky man followed her around. Unfortunately, there was only one other customer in the store.

"Yeah, well, I'm thinking about getting a second pair, just in case."

"A very wise idea, young lady. May I see your current pair?"

Uh-oh. Bad move, Weiss. "Oh, gee, I forgot to bring them. I only use them for reading, see, and I just came from school, and they're at home," she blurted out. "So I'll just look today, and if I like something, I'll come back with the other glasses so you can take the prescription off them. OK?" she finished hopefully.

"That's fine with me," the salesman said. "You just pick what you like, and I'll show you to one of our video booths."

"Great." Carole snatched at the first ten frames near her, picking some rimless ones, some heart-shaped ones, and a pair you could twist like a pretzel and never break. The salesman showed her to a small, windowless cubicle in the back of the store.

"It's very simple to operate this gizmo," he explained, turning on the machine. "You see, I just flip this switch, and you're on 'Candid Camera.' " He fiddled with a few dials to bring the picture into focus. "Now just take your time." He smiled.

"I certainly will," Carole sang out, when he had closed the door behind him. She laid the glasses in a line in front of her and peered up at the camera.

Her teeth looked very long to her when she smiled, sort of wolflike. She wiped the smile off her face and gazed intently into the screen. There, that was better.

"Fellow students," she began softly. "I guess you're all wondering why I called you here today." Then she giggled, noticing that when she spoke seriously, she tended to raise one eyebrow. She wasn't sure, but she thought that made her look insincere.

"I'd like to talk to you today about the senior lounge," she said, in a declamatory tone. The video screen reflected her hands moving jerkily in rhythm with her words. That was ghastly! She remembered seeing politicians on TV waving their arms around like flags, detracting from whatever they were saying. One firm, clear movement was worth a thousand jerks.

"We need a senior lounge, and it's going to be a project we can all get behind." Was her voice too nasal? Too squeaky? She should have brought Dave along to criticize her. It was one thing to see yourself on camera, but you could never really tell what your own voice sounded like, until you heard it on a tape recorder. She concentrated on lowering her voice, making it ring with meaning and emotion.

"Senior . . . lounge!" she announced. No, that was all wrong. She tried another approach.

"Steve," she said more softly to the camera, "if you're out there, I'd like to address my next remarks to you." Hmm, that was pretty good, emotional but completely believable. "You know how much I admire the work you've done for Twain High over the years, but it's time for a change now. I think a woman as president of the senior class would be good for our school, for you, and for everyone else."

This was weird! When she pretended she was

talking to Steve, she sounded serious, as if she meant every word. And she did. Nothing about it was phony. She propped her elbows on the counter in front of her and rested her head in her hands. Had she been lying to herself all along? Was everybody right about her feelings, and was she full of it?

The Carole who stared back at her from the video camera was definitely softer than she liked to think of herself. She had nice eyes and a pretty good nose, and she wasn't anything like the tough cookie she imagined herself to be. She didn't hate Steve! Actually, he was part of what made her tick. All her anger toward her parents, toward grown-ups in general, had something to do with the way she felt about Steve. She sat staring at herself, wondering why it had taken her so long to be honest about her feelings. Every time she got mad at Steve, why that was only because she cared so much. And when he was so stiff and formal, she felt left out, because she really wanted him to let down his guard with her. Of course! And probably the closer they got—if they ever did get close again—the more arguments they'd have. But that was OK, too. It was just part of a normal relationship.

"And in conclusion," she said quietly, in a mellow, low voice that she didn't even know she had, "I have to say that I'll run as hard and as fast as I know how for this position, but I'll never do anything to hurt you—ever."

She leaned back and sighed, just as she heard a tap at the door. The salesman stuck his head in.

"Don't mean to rush you. I just thought I'd see if you'd found anything you liked."

"As a matter of fact"—Carole grinned at him, sweeping all the glasses frames off the counter into her lap—"I really did."

"Well, that's fine," the man nodded. "And which will it be?"

"The ones that make me look most like myself—don't you agree?" She picked up one at random, a huge pair of deep red frames, and stuck them on her nose. Then she giggled. "I think I better ask my mother's opinion, though. I'll bring her when I bring the prescription." She handed all the frames back to the man, who was certain he'd made a sale.

"But I want to thank you for this opportunity," Carole said, in her best nominee's voice. "It's been *swell*."

On Saturday Mary Ann borrowed her mother's car so that she and Carole could "make the rounds" as she put it.

"But what good is this going to do?" Carole frowned, staring glumly out the car window at the beautiful weather. "It seems pushy to go around to people's houses and bang on doors."

"It *is* pushy, that's the whole point." Mary Ann sighed. "You have to make a splash and show you're different from all the other candidates."

"I already am." Carole grimaced. "Nobody else plays the guitar."

Mary Ann looked straight ahead at the road. "I will not argue about this. We've already discussed the fact that being the leader of Plant Life is not your strongest suit. A lot of people think rock is frivolous."

"Yeah, and a lot of people don't take the threat of nuclear war seriously. That doesn't make them right."

"Carole," Mary Ann said. "Shut up."

They covered West Hartford first. Mary Ann was ecstatic—because of the weather, everybody was out working on their cars or shooting baskets or helping their fathers clean out the garage.

"Hi, Tom!" Mary Ann yelled to one of their classmates, pulling over to the curb. She gave Carole a look that said, "You're on," and turned off the ignition.

"How're you doin', girls?" Tom grinned. He was polishing his bicycle.

"Got a minute, Tom?" Carole smiled, turning on the charm. *You're talking to Steve, remember!*

"What can I do for you this gorgeous day?"

Carole cleared her throat. "Well, it's about the election. I'm—"

"Oh, hey, sure, where do you want me to sign?" He stood up and reached for the petition Mary Ann had on her clipboard.

"Well, that was easy," Carole muttered.

"Hey," he said, signing his name with a flourish, "I'm for Sally Scott all the way, but I've got nothing against other people running."

"Oh, great," said Mary Ann sarcastically under her breath.

"Thanks," Carole said. "See you, Tom." She wandered back to the car, and Mary Ann was right behind her. They each climbed in and closed their doors.

"Next!" Carole said to her friend as they drove off.

The next hour and a half was a dizzying round of avoiding mothers with sodas and cookies, trying to get guys to stop playing ball and telling awful jokes, and meeting the disapproving stares of at least ten girls they weren't friendly with. They got signatures all right, but their moods grew progressively bleaker as they realized that a name on a piece of paper was not a commitment to vote.

"I think you should talk more and promise more," Mary Ann coached Carole as they pulled into the lot behind McDonald's. "You're too wishy-washy."

Carole groaned and got out of the car for what seemed like the hundredth time that day.

"Please, Mary Ann, I'm a sensitive person, you know. I can't force anything."

"I'm not asking you to stuff the ballot box, you nerd. I just want you to push yourself, that's all."

"Yeah, yeah." They opened the door of the restaurant, and Carole drew back with a sharp intake of breath when she saw who was seated at a center table surrounded by a crowd of about twenty kids. It was Steve. Nobody glanced up as the two girls came in.

"Want a Coke?" Mary Ann grumbled, looking angrily at the table full of Landyites.

"Not particularly." Carole hesitated only a moment before plunging into the fray. Hadn't this been what she'd wanted all along? To talk as if she were talking directly to Steve? Well, here he was.

"Because our school, unlike others in Hartford, has a sense of cooperation," she heard Steve saying as she came closer, "the kids want to get behind each other for a common goal."

"Naturally, it depends on the goal," Carole cut in quickly from the sidelines. Everyone looked up, and Steve froze, but only for a second. "Hey, Carole, Mary Ann, how's it going?"

"Just fine, thanks." Carole nodded at the group, taking in the familiar faces. She'd been hoping for some of those votes herself, and she wasn't about to give them up.

"Listen, we didn't mean to interrupt," Mary

Ann cut in, yanking Carole by one arm. The message was clear—you don't cut in on someone else's territory once they've staked it out.

"OK, so take it easy everyone." Carole smiled genially.

"Catch you later," Steve said, a look of relief spreading across his face as they walked away.

Carole didn't speak until they were back at the car. "Phooey!" she exploded. "Did you see Laurie and Denise? They were hanging on his every syllable. I was sure they'd vote for me."

"Nothing's sure at this stage, Carole. Look, the one good thing about running into Steve here is that we get to cover the mall. Connie might be there or Sally, but we'll just go where they're not. What are we waiting for?"

She scooted behind the wheel, and they took off like a shot. Carole sank down in her seat and gave a deep sigh. It wasn't so much a sigh of hopelessness as it was of loss. Each time she actually saw herself in competition with Steve, it got tougher.

"Do you think I have a chance? Be honest, now," she said seriously, glancing down at the list on Mary Ann's clipboard.

"Until the last ballot is counted, you have a darn good chance!" her friend declared, swinging up to the entrance of the East River Mall. It was just three o'clock, a perfect time to snag the crowd at the video arcade. Although Carole begged for a quick burger first, Mary Ann was adamant. "You don't deserve to fill your stomach until you've done your work," said the cruel taskmaster. "There they are!"

A group of fifteen juniors hovered over the video games, muscling out the little kids, who jingled their quarters hopefully each time a game ended. Carole was not really friendly with any of these potential constituents, and she was eager to get over to the clothing boutiques, where she knew many of her friends hung out and window-shopped each Saturday.

Mary Ann greeted the video fanatics with hearty hellos. She wasted no time and pushed Carole forward.

"Hi, guys," Carole began for the zillionth time that day. "I'm running for senior class president, as you well know, and I'm here to tell you why you ought to sign this petition and preserve democracy at Twain High."

She kept talking, trying to vary the pitch and tone of her voice, as Mary Ann circulated, pressing her pen into any free hand not clamped to a machine control. The great thing about getting these signatures was that real video freaks had no trouble concentrating on the game and signing away their life at the same time. When you nabbed a crazed player, you didn't have to worry about your powers of persuasion. He or she wasn't listening anyway.

"And in conclusion," Carole droned, suppressing a giggle as she watched Mary Ann help a wild-eyed player scrawl his name with his left hand, "I'd like to say that if I have my way, I'll make certain that a video machine is installed in our senior lounge, with one free game given away at random once a day."

Mary Ann's mouth dropped open, but Carole put a finger to her lips as she stole quietly away and urged her friend to follow. These guys might be dumb, but they weren't stupid enough to believe a lie like that. It was just a good closing remark, was how she saw it. Politicians always threw in something for effect.

"Uh-oh, it's Connie." Mary Ann pointed just past the frozen yogurt shop. Sure enough, there she was, talking to about ten kids. They were all laughing about something. Mary Ann pulled Carole down the escalator and scarcely acknowledged their next nemesis, who was riding the up escalator with five of his friends. It was Michael Brooks. The place seemed to be swarming with candidates.

With a thudding heart, Carole examined the clipboard, while they walked slowly to Fashion Alley, the best part of the mall. They had only twelve signatures to go! It had been a pretty profitable day after all.

"I'm exhausted," Carole gasped, flopping onto one of the benches lining the mall's spurting fountain.

"It's hard work," Mary Ann admitted, grabbing Carole's hand and pulling her upright.

"But we can't stop now. It's like lying down in the middle of a blizzard. You might close your eyes and never get up again."

"What I love about you," Carole said, laughing and giving Mary Ann a playful punch, "is you always look on the bright side."

"Oh, look, oh, this is great!" Mary Ann pointed down the alley at Sally Scott, who was standing with a group of girls in front of the Singer Sewing Center. They crept closer, until they could hear Sally's monotonous voice reciting a grocery list of wonderful things she was going to do if she was elected. The other girls listened politely, several of them shifting from foot to foot.

"And if you have any questions," Sally finished, looking over the heads of those closest to her, "I wish you'd stick around. I'll be right back—just want to make a quick trip to the ladies' room."

"I have this wonderful idea," Mary Ann said, chuckling. "C'mon!" She led Carole around the bend to the ladies' room and rushed her inside.

"What the—?" Carole frowned.

"I've wanted to try this for years." Mary Ann walked into a stall in the deserted room and closed it behind her. Carole heard the bolt slide into place. Then there was silence.

Suddenly Mary Ann's head appeared from under the door, and she crawled out. "Hurry up! Help me!" She started on the next stall.

"You nut! What are you doing?"

"Will you help me? We haven't got much time."

She locked the second and third stalls and was at the mirror combing her hair when Sally walked in. Carole began fumbling in her pocketbook for something—anything. She glanced over at Mary Ann who, with a completely straight face, was winding her silky red hair into a bun.

Mary Ann nodded. "Hi, Sally."

"Hi," Carole added hastily, about to burst out laughing.

Sally said a quick hello to them and went directly to the first stall. She pushed at it gingerly and frowned before going on to the next one. When she was again unsuccessful, she shook her head and moved on to the third. Zilch.

"Oh, well. . . ." she muttered, trying the first two again, just in case. "How stupid. I just hate this. They really ought to take better care of these places."

"I couldn't agree more," Mary Ann told her, not even watching as Sally dashed out the door, clearly in desperate need of another bathroom.

Carole stared at her friend. "You've got a mean streak, do you know that? That's plain nasty."

"Just a little practical joke." Mary Ann giggled, putting her comb back into her pocketbook. "You know how I love them."

Carole moaned in exasperation as three little old ladies wandered into the bathroom. "Oh, hello." Mary Ann smiled nervously at them.

"Wait just a sec," Carole told them, getting down on her hands and knees and crawling under the first door. "They just fixed these, see," she called to the three puzzled women. "But they forgot to unlock the doors."

"There's nothing wrong with them, really," Mary Ann reassured them, crawling under the next door to open it.

When they emerged, the women had vanished. Carole and Mary Ann looked at each other and realized how ridiculous they must have looked. Their laughter, starting as choked wheezes and guffaws, became a riotous bout of hysterics. Eventually they had to hold onto each other for support.

"Grow up, will you?" Carole chided her friend between belly laughs. She wiped the tears from her eyes, but more came.

"Me?" Mary Ann shouted. "I don't have to grow up. *You're* the one who wants to be president."

"Heaven help me!"

Then they started laughing all over again.

Chapter Six

On Monday after school, all the candidates were asked to meet with Mr. Schlesinger and a faculty committee to go over the basics of running a good, clean election. Carole listened with a barely suppressed yawn on her lips, but she was polite, having vowed to give grown-ups a second chance every time she felt they were doing something dumb. She'd always liked Mr. Schlesinger a lot because he had a quick sense of humor that matched her own. As for the other teachers, well, she was beginning to think that some of them were all right.

She was enormously relieved that her petition of signatures was complete, since today was the due date. More than one candidate in years past had been scratched by the faculty for lack of student support.

As she glanced around the room, she noticed that Sally, Bobby, and Melissa were listening to

Mrs. Johnson, one of the history teachers, as though she were the source of all wisdom, and Spike had worn a tie and jacket to school! Even Steve didn't do that. Pete Kelly looked pretty glum, but everyone knew that he really wasn't in the running for president. He was hoping for a lower spot, particularly the job of treasurer because he could do that best. Michael seemed sort of bored, as if he knew it all, and Connie was tapping her nails on the arm of her chair.

"OK, kids, I think that's about it," Mr. Schlesinger concluded at about four-thirty. "I just want to stress, since nobody else will, that this election, although important, is not the beginning or end of your young lives. If you make it, great; if you don't, you will undoubtedly find dozens of other ways to keep busy throughout your senior year."

He eased his ample form out of the desk seat and rubbed his forehead thoughtfully. For the first time that afternoon, Carole found herself listening intently.

"Have you noticed," he went on, "how all this—the campaign, the platforms you are adopting—is teaching you about real life but somehow still smacks of unreality? Think about it." He searched each of their faces, his electric-blue eyes meeting theirs.

"You mean," Steve cut in, "that even when one of us gets to be president, it's still just a school election."

Mr. Schlesinger nodded. "Exactly. Now this is not to say you shouldn't work yourselves silly to get picked, and it doesn't mean it's not a vital and responsible set of jobs, but. . . ." He paused a moment, considering what he wanted to tell them. "But if you don't make it this time, that's not to say you can't go into politics when you're older, if you have your heart set on it. It's also a fact that most high-school officers never do anything with politics later on. Getting the job shows they're natural leaders, but that could be helpful in any field—business, administration, the arts, the sciences. This is good preparation for your future, you see, but not necessarily in the way you think it's going to be."

Mrs. Johnson shifted uncomfortably in her seat. "On the other hand," she said in her high-pitched voice, "we're talking about the present and how important that is. So go out there and compete! That's the only way to win."

Carole shook her head at the woman. Hadn't she understood a thing Mr. Schlesinger had said? He made so much sense, she thought as she gathered up her things and followed the others out the door. He was definitely a grown-up with smarts, someone worth listening to.

She was standing in the corridor in pensive silence when she felt a hand on her arm. The other candidates and the teachers had all gone their separate ways, and there was only one other person who'd stuck around. It was Steve.

"Hi," he said, smiling down at her. She glanced up and remembered suddenly all those times after school, all those lovely long afternoons they had spent together. She felt a pang of sadness but quickly pushed it away. "Hi," she said cheerily.

"You rushing off to write a position paper, or could I entice you with a nice, cold Coke?"

"What for?" she asked suspiciously.

"Hey!" He raised his hands in protest. "It's not like a date or anything, Carole. I just thought you might like to discuss things, you know, talk business. Mr. Schlesinger said a lot of important stuff—I guess my head is kind of filled up with it."

"Yeah," she acknowledged. "Mine, too."

They stared at each other for a minute, sizing each other up as worthy adversaries, as lost partners, as two people in the same situation, who definitely could use some mutual support.

"OK," she said at last.

To her great relief, he didn't suggest their old hangout, Amy's, but led her to his beat-up VW Bug and drove her out to Sisson Avenue. Carole closed her eyes as they sped along the highway, enjoying the feeling of going somewhere with a guy. It had been so long! Then she told herself to snap out of it. She sat up straighter in her seat.

The coffee shop was nearly empty except for a few truck drivers and two women having an early supper together. Steve led Carole to a table in the back and surprised her by pulling out the chair for her. She was reminded of a few romantic dinners they'd had together in the past.

"So." He cleared his throat. "You got all your signatures?" The waitress came over with menus, and Steve quickly ordered Cokes for both of them.

Carole shrugged. "Getting the names was easy. It's everything else that's hard."

"Right!" Steve agreed. Then there was silence. "So, how're your folks?" he asked, somewhat nervously, Carole thought.

"They're fine," she told him. "Yours?"

"Fine. Carole. . . ." He leaned back in his chair and stretched out his long legs. They bumped hers by accident. "Oh, sorry!" he exclaimed, pulling away. Then he smiled nervously. "This is the most difficult thing I've ever done."

She looked at him, amazed at his honesty. "It's not so easy for me, either. I don't really know why you asked me." But she did know, and it gave her a nice, warm feeling inside that he'd cared enough to pursue her, even after she'd said no once.

"Well, I can't really talk to Spike or Melissa—certainly not to Sally or Michael or the others. I feel like one man against the world."

"You do!" Carole examined his strong, angular face, his clear brown eyes, his neatly parted chestnut hair. "Steve, it's hard to believe you're really all worked up over this election. I mean, you've been in the thick of school politics right along. Unlike me," she said, laughing.

"But something's changed," he admitted. "Oh, I suppose I shouldn't be telling you, a fellow competitor, as Mrs. Johnson would put it, but I never actually thought about what I wanted. Until now, that is." He gave her a meaningful look, and she could feel the blush start around her hairline and travel down to her neck.

"What do you mean?" She was relieved to see the waitress appear with their Cokes, and she made a fuss of tearing the wrapper off her straw so that she wouldn't have to look at Steve.

"Well, before, I got involved in things because everyone expected me to. My father particularly. You know how lawyers are." Steve shook his head. "Real interested in my developing 'leadership qualities.' He basically pushed me into extracurriculars freshman year, and after that I had all these"—he sighed, a bit uncomfortable with his confession—"expectations to live up to. I've just discovered I was thinking the way other people wanted me to." He ran a hand through his hair, unconsciously making it less neat. "I don't want to do that anymore."

Carole felt herself getting all soft and sympathetic, which put her back on guard. "You sound like you don't want to be president. Maybe you should step down," she suggested.

"I never said *that!*" he snapped at her. Then, seeing that his tone had upset her, he added, "But you ought to see Sally Scott in action. The girl is determined, you have to hand her that. She's got color-coded files, she's got an entire staff of kids working for her, she had her father print up these fliers for her—I don't know. It just tires me out watching her in action—and we haven't seen the half of it. I understand she's got other strategies, too." He drank half his Coke in one long gulp, and then he went on. "It's also what Mr. Schlesinger said. It really got to me. The election is sort of unreal when you think about it."

Carole took a sip of her Coke. "No more unreal than my playing in a rock group. I mean, I get a kick out of it and so do the rest of the girls, but that doesn't mean we're going to end up as the next Fleetwood Mac. Steve," she said earnestly, "it's silly to say that what we do doesn't count because we're only teenagers. That's how *they* see it. We're people, too, just like them, only with less power."

He frowned, and then finally, he nodded slowly. "I'd forgotten how logical you were. How much sense you can make."

She pushed her Coke away nervously, not sure what to say next. "Listen, this has been great, OK, but I've got to get home now."

"Me, too." He reached in his pocket for his wallet, and at the same time she dug a dollar out of her jeans pocket and slapped it on the table. "Hey," he objected. "I invited you."

"I can pay for myself," she said rather huffily. "Anyhow, you said this wasn't a date."

"Still the same feisty little Carole," he grumbled. "Still have to do everything yourself."

"Yup." She got up and started for the door.

"But when I *do* take you out on a date—which I intend to do before very long," he said, taking her arm, "then I pay."

"We'll see about that." It occurred to her that she hadn't enjoyed talking to anybody so much in a very long time. It was fun to argue with Dave, and Mary Ann's practical jokes were great, but there was no one who made her feel so special, so smart and important, as Steve did. Part of her held back from feeling so strongly, because it had only gotten her into trouble before. But another part of her said, go ahead, let it happen if it's going to. As she walked out of the coffee shop, she decided to give her confusion time to clear up. Everything got better if you gave it enough time.

"I'll have you home in a sec," Steve promised. "And won't your mother be surprised to see us driving up to your front door together."

"Oh, gosh," Carole exclaimed, rolling her eyes at the thought of all her mother's questions

104

about Steve after he had called. "Maybe you'd better leave me at the corner."

"Nice." Steve started up the car and looked over at her. "Ashamed to be seen with me, huh?"

"It's not that," Carole protested. "It's just . . . she can really give me a hard time about certain things."

"Like about me?" Steve wouldn't let her off the hook.

"No!" Carole felt her face getting red all over again. "She's just my mother, OK, and she has a few pet peeves, among which boys rank highest. My music runs a close second." She sighed and shifted in her seat, watching the traffic light turn green as though her life depended on it. "Just take me home, would you, Steve?"

"No problem." They drove along in silence for several minutes, and then Steve said, "But do *you* really want to be president?"

"Sure I do," Carole answered, too quickly.

"Why? And don't give me that bit about how the school needs a change of pace. You're running just to get close to me again, aren't you?"

She turned around in shock, her jaw dropping open. "How dare you say a thing like that?"

"Because I know you a little," he answered smugly.

"You don't know *beans!*" She folded her arms across her chest and was stonily silent the rest of the way home. She wouldn't even give him a civil answer about his coaching her for the campaign but simply insisted he leave her off half a block from her house.

She didn't bother to look back when she stormed out of his car minutes later, but she couldn't miss his words. "If neither of us wins, I'll still love ya!" he called, and there was laughter in his voice.

A lot he knows, she fumed to herself as she went into the house. But her heart was beating a little bit faster. Did she want to go along with Steve's plans for the two of them? And if she did, would she be sorry?

For the next week Carole didn't have a free minute. She spoke on the school radio program, "Around Twain." Then she let it be known that she would be available each afternoon after school to answer questions. She monitored the other candidates carefully and made Mary Ann her official spy. If Sally Scott was doing a telephone blitz after school and sending out fliers to every member of their class, Carole wanted to know about it so she could go her one better. If Steve was actively soliciting votes at Amy's, she would pick another hangout and stay twice as long. Her parents watched her growing fervor with interest, and slowly they came around to her side. Each night they offered more sympathy and support, and Carole was grateful to have it. Campaigning was exhausting but seemed to be worthwhile.

About ten days after the campaign got under

way, there was a notice on the bulletin board outside the faculty lounge. Dave was assigning profiles of the candidates to six of his most trusted reporters. Carole took a deep breath and marched downstairs to the newsroom. The big freeze between Dave and her had gone on far too long, and it was up to her to do something about it.

"No, that's no good!" Dave flapped some typewritten pages in front of a very disgruntled Andy Peterson, the sports page editor. "I'm telling you for the last time, you're skating on real thin ice."

Carole stood quietly in a corner, watching the mayhem. Seeing Dave in action, she realized how much she missed his spunk.

Dave noticed her, and she started toward him, praying that he wouldn't give her the cold shoulder. He met her gaze as she walked across the room, but then at the last moment he turned away, pulling his cap down over his eyes.

"Can I talk to you?" Carole asked.

"Shoot. But I don't have much time to kill," he said dismissively.

"Me neither." She wedged herself onto a corner of his crowded desk and sat down, her legs swinging in front of her. "Look, I just wanted to ask you if I can write my own interview. You know I'm a good writer, and I know a lot more about me than any reporter."

He swung around and picked up one side of

his visor so he could peer at her quizzically with one eye. "What do you mean?"

"I want to write questions and answers for candidate Carole Weiss is what I mean. I promise to be fair and impartial."

He frowned, then turned away again. "Suit yourself."

"Dave?" Her tone was pleading now. "Would you quit the nastiness? This is your old buddy, Carole, remember? Hey," she continued, when he just stared at her and said nothing, "I'm talking to you."

"And I'm telling you to give it up. That's about the most honest anybody's gonna be with you."

"Well, I won't give up. Listen"—she edged closer to him and lowered her voice—"I don't know if I have a chance, but I want to try to get through to everyone that my platform is going to make a difference. I want people to feel that they have a voice in what's going on, and I want them to dive in and do their part, too." Carole went on, trying to make Dave understand. "I've been working out my ideas for students' rights and volunteer work. I'm concerned about issues, not dances. . . ."

"Whooee!" Dave gave a long whistle. "You sure aren't running on the popularity ticket, are you? Hey, it's all well and good for you to think up real issues, but how are you going to get votes on a program of senior volunteer work? Sweetheart, all seniors want to do is cut classes and go hang out in the parking lot."

"Well, I'm doing my best. But I'd feel better if I knew I still had your support as a friend."

"I'll think about it," Dave said after a minute. "Give me some time, OK?"

"You're great!" She threw her arms around him in a fierce bear hug. "All's forgiven?" she asked.

"Yeah, sure," he nodded, pushing her away awkwardly. "You just got me really mad, you know. But I guess I'd rather have you in power than any of those other creeps. Just remember one thing—I'm betting on you to lose and lose big. So I'll stick by you because you know I always root for the underdog. And believe me, Carole, you are *under* the underdog."

"We'll see." Carole laughed, starting for the door. "I'll turn in my interview next week sometime."

"Tuesday!" he yelled as she barged out the door.

Carole was grinning when she ran to the corner to catch the bus. She knew the rest of the group would already be at Janice's warming up for the rehearsal, but it was crucial that she get Dave on her side. The time had been well spent. Besides, his friendship and support meant a lot to her, and she hated to think that she might have turned him off. For all his tough talk, he didn't have a lot of friends because he pretended to prefer being a loner.

The bus stopped at the corner of Asylum and Maple, and she jumped out, making directly for the Brunos' house. It was a beautiful afternoon, perfect for sitting out on a porch and just enjoying spring. What was Steve doing right now? she wondered dreamily, as she climbed the steps and rang the bell. She'd only run into him a couple of times over the past week, and although he'd been friendly, he hadn't mentioned a thing about a date. Carole was getting antsy enough to ask him out—just to talk about the school election assembly, of course, nothing more serious than that.

Oh, dry up, Weiss! she chided herself. You've got romance on the brain and don't deny it!

Mrs. Bruno let Carole in, and when she ran down the stairs to the basement, the other girls glared at her stonily.

"You're late," Mary Ann pointed out needlessly from her seat at the small electric keyboard.

"I thought we agreed to take this thing seriously, Carole," Ellen said angrily.

"I'm here now, and that's the most important thing," Carole said calmly, using Lesson One from *Improving Your Powers of Persuasion*. The great thing about preparing for this election was that it carried over into other areas. She grabbed her guitar from its place in the corner and started tuning.

"Well, as I was saying, Alice," Ellen said, still looking in Carole's direction, "if we're going to go for that key change right after the sixteenth bar, I don't want any drums in there confusing me. I need to think about the notes."

Alice did a quick roll on the snare and then hit the cymbal. "Just this much, Ellen. Don't be so picky."

"I think Alice is right," Janice pointed out. "Nobody's going to get the excitement of the change in key, if the drum doesn't punch it."

"Let's try it both ways," Carole suggested, taking her place in between Janice and Ellen. "See what sounds best."

"Spoken like a true politician." Ellen sneered, planting her hands on her hips. She was very tall, almost as tall as Steve, and Carole had always felt like a shrimp when Ellen talked down to her. Today, though, things were different. She felt secure and sure of herself.

"I suppose," Carole agreed. "But let's give it a go. Talking won't solve anything." She pointed back at Alice. "A—one, a—two, a—one—two—three—four. . . ."

They took it from the top in a rocking number called "Be My Guy," a song Carole had written some months ago. It had a good beat, but not much else—even Carole could tell that. When they got to the break, she stopped them and said to Ellen, "Why don't you wail a little here? No lyrics. That'll give Alice a chance to pick up the tempo. When you come out of that part, you'll be in the next key, and you can start singing again. How's that?"

"Brilliant!" Mary Ann shouted.

"I'm not sure," Ellen mumbled, but she nodded when Alice went back and started over. They tried it, and it worked. Carole felt pretty smug that her tactic had worked—so smart, as a matter of fact, that she didn't feel the need to say anything about the next number, a slow ballad that was basically a set piece for Ellen's deep, rich voice.

The third piece they rehearsed was kind of a mess because neither Carole nor Janice had practiced it, and they missed notes every other phrase. "Wow, that's really poor," Mary Ann grumbled.

"We'll work on it," Janice snapped, wiping sweat from the nape of her neck. They'd been at it now for only half an hour, but it was exhausting work. "How about a break?" Janice suggested.

"Hey, c'mon!" Mary Ann protested. "We don't have that much time. Our first gig is, what's the date, Ellen?"

"May ninth, and I've firmed it up. My aunt's church bazaar is generally packed with all kinds of people, so it's a perfect showcase for us."

"Oh, hey," Carole interrupted. "I meant to discuss that with you guys. I just won't be able to make rehearsals the week before that. I think we'd better cancel the bazaar."

The other four girls stared at her in disbelief. "You'll make it," Ellen stated at last, "if I have to drag you to every single rehearsal by your hair."

"Look, I'm sorry, but the election's on the seventh. Do you realize how swamped I'm going to be?"

"Tough." Alice, usually the quiet one, sounded like she meant business.

Carole looked to Mary Ann for support and was startled to see the grim, determined look on her friend's face. "Plant Life was born before you got this yen to run for public office, Carole. And it seems to me you can make time for things you want to do. Think about it."

A heavy silence hung in the room. Everyone was down on her now, and she realized they had a point, a very good point. She couldn't let her friends down.

"Let's try the punk number." Janice sighed, tightening one of her guitar strings. "We never do that one right."

Alice gave them the beat, and they plunged in again. Carole played loudly, trying to drown out the plaintive cries of her own conscience. Sometimes life was just too complicated.

Chapter Seven

"It was only because I knew you weren't serious about canceling the gig that I didn't rush to your defense," Mary Ann explained. Carole, seated at her cluttered desk in her bedroom, was only half-listening. She was desperately trying to get her thoughts straight for her platform speech.

"Huh?" She chewed distractedly on a piece of her hair. "I was serious."

"No, Carole," Mary Ann stated flatly, throwing herself across Carole's bed, "you were just preoccupied. But I've solved the whole thing, so you can get all ready for the election and still devote practically all of your time to Plant Life. Maybe even have a little bit left over for Steve." She giggled.

"MA, you're taking up precious moments. I've got carloads of homework, I have to write my piece for Dave, and practice my speech for the assembly, which is in less than two weeks. How can I possibly—?"

"Carole, will you give me a second?" Mary Ann rolled over on her back and crossed one leg over her knee. "The election's in the bag. I have a way for you to win friends and influence people."

"Yeah?" Carole asked suspiciously. "What'd you have in mind—bribery?"

"Not exactly." Mary Ann sat up, a wide grin spreading across her face. "We'll give a big party. You invite everybody—not just the music crowd. None of the other candidates, of course, but the newspaper people and jocks and grinds and nerds. Everybody!"

"Well," Carole mused, "it sounds interesting, sure, but I don't like this monopolizing the limelight. What about having all the candidates— show everyone what a good person I am, to have my worst adversaries right in my own living room, eating my own sandwiches?"

"Hmmm." Mary Ann nodded. "I like it. It's different—daring even. You must admit it's a brilliant notion, Carole. You get the whole gang on *your* turf, fill them up with food, soda, and good music, and you've as good as won. You know all these fund-raiser parties the senators and mayors and city councilmen throw? It's done all the time—an excellent forum for any serious candidate."

"Well. . . ." Carole took another strand of her hair and stuck it in her mouth.

"If you really wanted to be president, you'd adopt a more conservative image," Mary Ann said.

"There's campaigning and then there's compromise," Carole announced. "I'm not going to change my image just to be president. What makes you think a traditional president is what our senior class wants?"

Mary Ann shrugged. "Tradition. No guy without it ever won."

Carole laughed and rolled her eyes to the ceiling. "Tell me more about the party."

"It should be a terrific mixer, OK? Get everyone talking, discussing, arguing—and eating. Wonderful food and plenty of great records. And you have to wear something primo." Mary Ann dashed over to Carole's desk and foraged around for a blank piece of paper so she could make a list. "Now Sally's going to look pretty silly in the face of this superior entertainment, don't you think? Even Steve will pale in comparison."

"MA," Carole said laughing, "candidates don't get elected because they put out a nice spread and play good music. That's not what counts."

"It is to teenagers," her friend said sensibly. She wrote a few items on her list. "You get back to work on that speech. I'll take care of the details."

"What about my mother?"

117

"Oh, yeah, well, you take care of her. See you." And with that, she was out the door.

Carole sighed and looked down at the notes scattered on her desk. She knew perfectly well there was no surefire way to do anything, be it win an election or be Steve's girlfriend again—if that was what she wanted. But maybe MA had a point. She should mingle with people who weren't in her crowd, and a party would be a great way to do it. She put down her notes and went to deal with her mother. Maybe, just maybe, she'd find her in a great mood.

Carole was astonished and delighted when her mother said yes with scarcely a moment's hesitation. She and Mary Ann threw themselves into making preparations for the party, and they were still hard at work on it the following Saturday, which broke warm and sunny. It was only the third week in April, but the forsythia had emerged in yellow clusters, and a few reluctant daffodils had already raised their heads from their winter slumber. It felt like spring, even though there were still only a few green buds showing on the bushes and trees.

It was a great day for the car wash—Twain High's annual fund-raising event, which was usually a lot of fun. The week before, all the kids had run around town putting up fliers advertising the event to the community. Now, bright and early Saturday, the first shift would start

118

work. At three dollars a car, there was generally a hefty sum to be given to the charity of their choice by the end of the day.

Carole grabbed her grubbiest jeans, put on a green Lacoste T-shirt and a maroon sweatshirt over it, and selected a pair of white tube socks to go with her sneakers. Then she tied her hair back with a green and red scarf. Not exactly the height of fashion, but she looked ready for business. Anyway, Steve had seen her this way plenty of times in the past. She was secretly pleased that he was on her car-washing team, which meant they'd be together from nine to twelve. After that, anything was possible. And she was determined to invite him to the party before they went home that afternoon.

She downed a glass of orange juice and reluctantly agreed to a plain doughnut with her coffee to keep her going through the long morning.

"Tell you what," her father said, leaning over the paper to inspect his daughter's costume and grinning. "I'll make a bid of two-fifty for you to wash the Buick before you leave. OK—two-eighty, but not a penny more."

"Dad . . ." Carole grumbled, attempting to ignore him.

"Sweetie, just this once! Do I ever ask you? And since you're in a car-washing frame of mind. . . ."

"This is for charity, Dad," she explained patiently.

"And charity begins at home," her parents chimed in chorus.

"Oh, you two!" She shook her head disparagingly, but she couldn't help giggling at the same time. Her parents were pretty funny and not at all as awful as she used to think they were. Maybe she was growing up a little herself, she mused, as she swung her leg over the bike and pedaled away toward school.

The set-up crew was already filling buckets with water and soapsuds when Carole drove up, and there were big new sponges to make the job a bit easier. The hoses trailed around the side of the school building from the janitor's closet.

"Morning." She turned around to see Steve grinning at her. He was shiny, scrubbed clean from his morning shower, and looked wonderful even in his oldest chinos and faded denim jacket. She loved it when he didn't get all dressed up.

"Hi." She nodded casually. "Ready to buckle down?"

"As usual," he acknowledged, pretending to be hurt that she'd implied he wasn't always. "Hey, have you seen the show-off lately?"

"Who do you mean?"

"Sally, who else?" he muttered. "I can't believe she did it."

"Did what, Steve?" Carole was jostled by one of the set-up crew, who thrust a wet sponge

120

nto her hand and told her to get to work. The
ine of cars was growing slowly around the park-
ng lot.

"Sally had campaign buttons printed up,"
Steve explained, as they walked to the cars.
"Real big ones, with her picture on them, no
ess."

"Oh, no!" Carole followed him to the first car
and started scrubbing.

"Not only that. She even got little rulers done,
oo, that say: Sally Scott Goes the Distance.
Must have cost her father a bundle—you have
o have those things printed in bulk. I mean,
aminated *plastic*, for heaven's sake."

"Whew!" Carole pushed a straggly hair back
from her forehead and soaped up the windshield.
Just when she was so confident about the party,
this had to happen. "I suppose she's giving
them out to everybody, huh? This is really bad,
teve."

"You said it." He followed her with the hose
and sprayed the area she'd just soaped. "Well,
we can get by without cheap gimmicks. I mean,
I can," he corrected himself quickly.

"Sure. Me, too." Carole sneaked a look at him
and saw that he was blushing. He'd said "we!"
He included her in the battle against Sally. But
then, where did that leave the problem of one
of them beating the other? Suddenly, Carole
wished that she and Steve might *tie* for the
presidency. But the chances of that were slim.

It was quite possible, though, that they might both get some sort of post. She no longer wanted to show him up. Maybe, she thought, just maybe, they'd learn to cooperate, now that she was sure he really respected her. And, of course, she did think that he had a lot of good ideas— when she was willing to admit it to herself. Working with him could turn out to be very different than she had originally thought. Much better.

The next two hours went by like nothing at all. The work became completely routine, and Carole welcomed the occasional spray from Steve's hose to take the edge off the sun's insistent rays. There was an easy rhythm to the soaping and rinsing and polishing, and a good feeling among all the kids. Even the usually grumpy adults, who came to have their cars washed, seemed cheery today.

Carole was really enjoying herself, horsing around with Max, Steve, and two other kids on their work team, Tanya and Paul, when something made her look up at the last car in line.

"What the—?"

"Yikes!" Steve dropped his sponge, and soapsuds splattered on everyone in the vicinity.

"Oh, boy," Tanya exclaimed, running a wet hand through her short, blond curls.

Carole quickly finished drying off the car she was working on and marched over to get a closer look. There, riding in style in her father's white

Ford Granada, was Sally Scott. The car was decorated with red streamers, and a large banner was draped across the back. It read: Sally Scott for Twain High Senior Class President. Sally was at the wheel, and every other seat but one was occupied by her supporters. In the back, chatting easily with the others, was Melissa Donleavy.

"Something strange is going on." Carole felt Steve at her right elbow, and she nodded her agreement, still unable to take her eyes off the campaign car. They were both drawn to it like moths to a flame. As they approached, Sally honked the horn.

"Hey, hi, you two. How's it going?" Irv Bates waved out the window. He was Sally's manager and had been practically glued to his candidate for the past three weeks.

"Just fine. We're working away," Steve muttered between clenched teeth. "Hi, Melissa," he added pointedly. Carole couldn't speak; she was simply paralyzed by the sight.

"Hello." Melissa smiled as if nothing unusual were going on.

"Surprised to see you here, Melissa," Steve went on, coming over to the side of the car.

"Yes, I suppose," she murmured.

"Go ahead, tell them," Eleanor Laiken prompted. She was Sally's best friend.

"Tell us what?" Carole asked suspiciously, finding her voice at last.

123

"Well. . . ." Melissa cleared her throat. "I'll be announcing it on Monday morning, so you might as well know now. I'm withdrawing from the election and throwing my support behind Sally."

"You're *what?!*" Steve practically fell over. "Oh, that's rotten. You're a creep, Melissa," he said, taken aback.

Carole would have laughed, if she hadn't been thinking the same thing herself. She had never heard Steve call anyone a creep—as a matter of fact, when they were going together, he used to criticize *her* for calling people names. To hear him say it sort of took the sting out of the hard truth that Sally, without even trying, had just been handed dozens of votes on a silver platter.

"I'm sorry you feel that way, Steve, but I had to go with my conscience. You ought to understand that." She leaned forward and tapped Sally on the shoulder. "I honestly feel that she's the best choice."

"Melissa," Steve said loudly, "don't count her votes before they're hatched, OK?" He walked over and waved the cars up in line. "Move it, Max," he shouted to his buddy.

Carole straggled after him, more confused than ever. What good was giving her big party if the odds were so stacked against her? And even Steve looked glum as they silently went back to work. It wasn't until the next work crew relieved them at noon that he spoke to her again.

"Let's get out of here," he suggested, rinsing

off his hands with the hose before handing it to Jimmy Bradshaw, who was taking over for him.

"Sure," Carole agreed. She went around to the side of the school and unlocked her bicycle, then wheeled it over to Steve, who was waiting for her. They walked down the drive and around the corner toward a quiet residential section. It was suddenly very still, the sounds of traffic rapidly diminishing as they walked along.

"Kind of bums you out, doesn't it?" Carole said at last.

"Melissa? Hey, forget about it," he said cheerily, reaching over to take one of her handlebars. "Remember her nomination speech? She just kept saying how sorry she was for all the things she hadn't done on all her committees this year. She couldn't have thrown that many votes toward Sally because I don't think she had that many to begin with. If it were Michael or Connie, maybe we'd have a problem, but not Melissa. Even Bobby Watson'll get more votes than she would have."

"Um," Carole murmured. The thing that depressed her more than the votes was something she didn't think she ought to mention. But one less candidate meant that much more of a struggle between her and Steve. She wasn't looking forward to May 7, even though seven had always been her lucky number.

"Say, I meant to ask you," she ventured, changing the subject quickly, "MA and I are

125

kind of giving a party next Saturday. You free by any chance?"

"Huh? Oh, I . . . yeah, I guess." He looked dumbfounded that she had invited him, and she hastily covered her embarrassment by saying, "It's a preelection bash. You know, *everyone*'ll be there."

"Sure. All right. Yeah, I think I can make it." He nodded, looking away. Was she imagining it, or did he seem to be disappointed that it wouldn't be a quiet little get-together?

"So what kind of chance do you think Spike has?" she asked absently, when Steve was silent for a few moments.

"About zero plus." He shrugged. "He was a write-off from the start."

"You don't think he could be a dark horse?" Carole asked hopefully. She hated the idea of Sally winning, was terribly nervous about winning herself, and had very mixed feelings about Steve. Michael had the makings of a good president, although his approach was a bit formal. Maybe Bobby, but he was so shy and uncomfortable speaking to people because of his stammer. And a president, as head of the senior class, needed to have a real presence. Now Connie had that, but Carole felt Connie didn't seem to care enough. And Pete, well, his forte was numbers. Carole wondered if he would draw enough votes to place as treasurer.

"No way, kid." Steve laughed, drawing Carole

out of her thoughts. He took the bike away from her and brought it around to his other side so that he could walk beside her.

Carole took off the scarf that had been holding her hair back and put it loosely around her neck. As she was running her fingers through her hair, a cool breeze sprang up suddenly, causing her scarf to flutter away.

"Hey!" Steve yelled, setting the bike down on the path and dashing after the green and red scarf, which flew swiftly in and out of the budding bushes. He finally pounced on it and lay sprawled in the grass, panting.

Carole quickly hopped on the bike and pedaled over to him, laughing. "Pretty klutzy, Steve!" she teased, flopping down beside him. She reached for the scarf, but he jerked it away playfully, taunting her by holding it just beyond her reach. He was so tall, he didn't have to work too hard to keep her at bay. When she lunged at him, determined not to be bested, he grabbed her arms and pinned them behind her. "You give?" he challenged her.

"Never!" She fought like a wildcat, but he was too strong for her. "Aargh! Lemme go!" As she thrashed to get away, she was suddenly aware of a feeling she'd never had before. There was a new thrill in this closeness, a sense that they belonged like this, laughing and happy together. Still, she wouldn't let herself relax and give up. It was too important that she show him how tough she was. No matter how she felt, she couldn't let him win. "Stephen!"

She dodged sideways and then switched back, but when he moved to pin her again, their heads collided with a loud crack.

"Ow! Oh, you killed me!" He rolled aside, clutching at his forehead with both hands.

"Ooh! Oh, I'm sorry. Did I hurt you?" Rubbing her own head, she reached over, a concerned look on her face. His crumpled expression of agony changed at once to one of tender amusement, and he grabbed at the hand she extended toward him, taking her delicate fingers and folding them into a ball inside his own huge hand.

"You're really something, you know that?" he whispered. "A worthy adversary."

"Yeah," she mumbled, her dark brown eyes fixed on his. "You're not so bad yourself."

Slowly she extended her fingers and intertwined them with his. They scrunched closer together in the grass, and his other hand began to creep around her shoulder. Something warm and meaningful passed between them, a look that made up for all their months of silence. Carole wished they could stay like that forever.

Suddenly a loud, grating voice jerked them both to attention. "Hey, you two! You gonna get that bike out of my rhododendrons, or what?"

Steve scrambled to his feet, yanking Carole along after him. "Really sorry," he babbled to the enraged home owner. "I don't think we did any damage, sir, but if we've broken any branches I'd be happy to pay you for your trouble."

The man growled under his breath, then waved them off in annoyance. "Naw, just get off my property, would you?"

Carole and Steve took the bike between them and left. But she couldn't stop a small smile of happiness from creeping across her face as they retreated down the block. How could she help it?—the warm feeling inside her was impossible to hide.

Chapter Eight

The night of the party was balmy and clear, the most beautiful April evening ever. Carole and Mary Ann worked all afternoon decorating the Weiss house and preparing the food, and Mrs. Weiss surprised them with a few batches of her wonderful carrot cake, which caused Carole to proclaim her mother "a real sport."

She and Mary Ann finished at about seven o'clock and then went upstairs to dress for the gala event.

"OK," Mary Ann said, heading straight for Carole's closet. "Now you've got to be the belle of the ball. We'll pick something great for you to wear, and then I'll take my shower and throw on the things I brought over."

"I'm glad you have this all organized," Carole said and chuckled.

"Well, who else is going to do it?" Mary Ann noisily pushed hangers aside. "Now, we need an outfit that absolutely screams self-confidence."

"How about my red jumpsuit with all the zippers?" Carole suggested. "That screams real loud."

"You're a riot. Just keep it up," Mary Ann grumbled, pulling out a dress to examine it. "You need the 'dressed for success' look, that's what you need. The sort of thing a business executive wears."

"A blue pin-striped suit is not appropriate for a party," Carole pointed out.

"Yes! Here it is! Perfect." Mary Ann pulled out a simple blue-and-white long-sleeved shirtwaist with a round collar.

"Bor-*ring!* Mary Ann, I haven't worn that in years."

"It's sedate, Carole. It's the statement of power and sensibility."

Carole stared at the dress, sizing it up. There was nothing creative or imaginative about its colors or lines. It was anti-everything Carole stood for. But on the other hand, it was possible that she didn't see herself the way others saw her. Really, could it hurt to wear it? Her friend seemed to think it was the key to a full ballot box. And she generally knew how to size up situations pretty well.

"Well, OK," agreed Carole, grabbing her bathrobe and starting for the shower. "I'll look like Sally."

"Exactly," declared Mary Ann as the door closed in her face.

Carole wore the dress. It didn't look *that* bad, and Mary Ann allowed her to put on a red belt and a red scarf to jazz it up. Carole told her friend she felt like the American flag, which prompted Mary Ann to say that she couldn't pick a better campaign strategy than patriotism. Carole didn't feel particularly patriotic, just a little nervous when the doorbell rang at seven forty-five.

"They aren't supposed to come till eight!" she complained, stumbling down the stairs with Mary Ann right behind her. But her mother beat her to the door. She was showing Dave inside, just as the two girls got to the front hallway.

"Nice to see you again, Dave," Mrs. Weiss said, grinning. "OK, you kids," she said directly to Carole. "I'm ducking into the den for the evening. Your father says to keep the volume down. And I say"—she winked at them—"have a ball!"

"You sure have a super mom," Dave declared, when Mrs. Weiss had disappeared. "I mean, she's not on your case all the time."

"Right," Carole nodded, feeling guilty for ever thinking badly of her mother.

"Hey, you look like a postage stamp." Dave chortled, slapping his thigh.

Mary Ann grabbed Carole by one arm and propelled her into the kitchen. "Don't even listen to him. What does he know?"

"I know what I see with my own eyes," Dave interjected, trailing behind them. "Whew! I don't know who dressed you up, Carole, but you don't look like you. If this election thing turns you into a clone, I'm giving up. You used to have a mind of your own, but now. . . ." He rolled his eyes to the ceiling despairingly.

"Nice of you to say so," Carole growled, shoving a plate of chips and dip at him. "Take this to the living room. Since you're early, you're going to work. And if you keep insulting me, I'll give you some more to do." She was cut to the quick by his comment. Was it true? If there was one thing she'd always prided herself on, it was not following trends that would brand her as a clone.

"Carole, I'm on your side," Dave protested, popping a handful of chips into his mouth. "Look, I came early to try to convince you to withdraw from the election."

"What!" Mary Ann screeched. "I don't want to hear this! Carole, don't listen," she repeated, and then under her breath she added, "Some friend he is."

"Mary Ann, you've got to look the truth square in the eye," Dave said. "Landy and Scott are going to tie up president and VP. The other spots aren't worth your time."

"Yeah? Well you just tell your crystal ball that it's dead wrong," Mary Ann said emphatically, whisking the plate of chips from Dave's hand, just as the doorbell rang again.

Carole smiled wryly at her good friend. From being a skeptical doubter, Mary Ann had turned around and become her best advocate. She told herself to calm down, stop thinking, and just enjoy herself.

By nine everyone had arrived except Sally and her crew, who had called to say they'd be late, and the party was in full swing. Everyone Carole had asked was there, which she took as a good sign. She figured that if they were convinced that she was going to lose the election, they would have stayed away in droves. Connie was dancing with Michael, something Carole found a little weird, and Bobby Watson had retreated to a corner to read a book.

Carole was busy putting sandwiches on a tray when a familiar voice startled her. Steve stood in the doorway of the kitchen, a glass of 7-Up in his hand.

"Well, hello! I haven't been able to get near you all night."

"Oh, sorry." Carole could see his interest in the warm, kind look he gave her. "I've been kind of frantic with all the people and everything, you know."

"Say, I really liked your piece in the *Herald*," he said emphatically, leading her out to a relatively quiet corner of the living room and seating her beside him. "It was an ingenious idea, really, to ask yourself those questions. I think you were more honest than you would have been if somebody else had been interviewing you."

"Your piece was excellent, too," Carole said, returning the support.

"Aw, I don't know. I tightened up when Joanie started on me. I guess I don't hold up too well under pressure."

"I think you do," Carole said.

"Well, it's nice of you to say so. Hey, your idea about the class trip and particularly about the elementary school lunch program is right on." He moved closer to her on the couch, and she could smell the tangy scent of his after-shave, the same one he used to wear when they were going out together. "If I'm elected, I think I may take a couple of your ideas—with your permission, of course, and with full credit to you," Steve went on.

Carole drew herself up, all traces of sentimental remembrance gone. "I wouldn't be too cocky about winning yet, Steve. I mean, all your ideas for senior class fund-raisers are good, but they don't have all *that* much substance. And the student-faculty discussion groups might work, maybe, but only if the right faculty will agree to come in on them. Seems to me you're counting on your debating background to move the masses over to your side. That's a long shot," she blurted, sidling one cushion away from him. How dare he suggest taking her platform and using it for his own purposes! "The voters have to feel you're going to deliver the goods."

His response was a quick, teasing smile. "Want to dance?" He got up and held out his arms. "Endless Love" was pouring through the stereo's speakers, and Carole knew she couldn't resist the pull of memory now. There was nothing as wonderful as dancing slow with Steve.

They were tentative at first, feeling their way back into each other's embrace. Carole kept a couple of inches between them and stared purposefully at Steve's shirt buttons, while their hands touched and his right arm came around her back. There, that was the way they used to do it. He was wearing a soft brown corduroy jacket and pressed brown gabardine slacks. His shirt was a neat, cream-colored button-down with thin red stripes. She knew each piece of his clothing—what it felt like, where it folded or creased on his long, lanky body. Being in his arms again was just like coming home after a long trip. It felt good.

"Look who just walked in," he murmured in her ear, after they had been dancing for endless minutes. "Sally and the gang."

"Huh?" She looked up, distracted from the grand feeling of cuddling in his arms and swaying against him. "Oh, yeah," she said, pulling away again. "They had someplace to go first. Campaign headquarters, I suppose." She nodded over to the tight group around Sally, which was herding her in just like sheepdogs around a prize lamb. Oblivious as she wanted to be to everything but her and Steve, Carole did notice that Sally looked particularly good. Her hair was pinned up on the sides with flowered combs, and she had on a simple lemon-yellow dress with three-quarter sleeves and a boat neck. She looked pretty good, Carole had to admit. But the interesting thing about Sally was that she hadn't changed her image for the occasion. She still looked like herself. Carole felt another pang of discomfort. What was she, some kind of hypocrite to do what Mary Ann told her to do and wear this stupid dress? What was at stake here, anyway? And how badly did she want to win? The price of glory could be pretty high—higher than she wanted to bid. Like losing Steve maybe. If she had him at all, that is.

"Shall we adjourn to your backyard for a Coke?" Steve asked her as soon as the song ended. He didn't wait for an answer but steered her firmly toward the kitchen, grabbing a couple of cans of soda as they went. Carole caught a glimpse of Mary Ann and Dave. They seemed to have everything under control, so she didn't protest. She and Steve went out the back door, and he closed it softly behind them.

"Nice night," he said casually, taking a seat on the top step.

"Perfect," she agreed, sitting on the one beneath him and glancing up at the moon, which was hiding coyly behind a cloud. "I love spring nights."

"I remember," he said, and then she felt the pressure of his hand on her shoulder. She was flooded with waves of caring and tenderness. For some reason, though, they were different from the feelings she'd had when they had danced together. Those had been thoughts from the past; these were of the present. It was *this* Steve she wanted to be close to, she thought suddenly. Now, as never before, they had a lot in common, a great deal to share.

His hand strayed to her shining dark hair, which fell softly to her shoulders. "Hey, I've missed you," Steve said softly.

She half-turned to him, a shy smile on her face. "I guess I feel about the same," she acknowledged. Her statement didn't sound terribly sincere, but after all, they were still competitors—she couldn't just fall in a heap at his feet.

"It seems to me we never appreciated each other before, Carole," he murmured. "We were always too busy fighting. But now it's better somehow. You know what I mean?"

"Uh-huh." She moved up a step to sit beside him. "You've loosened up since last year," she said, grinning, "and I have to admit it's a welcome change from the way you used to be."

"But you're the one who's different!" he exclaimed. "You used to be such a nut, you know?"

"Well, thanks a *lot!*"

"But a nice nut." He put an arm around her shoulder and drew her close. "I never really thought you'd have the guts and stamina to do something as conventional as run for senior class president."

"And I never thought you'd be as open to new ideas as you are." Carole turned in the circle of his arms, still ever so slightly wary of the physical contact between them. It had been so long, she had to ease back into it, sort of like into a tub of very hot water.

"Well, sure. I mean, you can be just so full of yourself on the debating team, but there's nothing at stake there—it's only throwing empty ideas around. But as senior president, you have to work for others. It's got to be more down to earth."

Carole looked away and licked her lips. "So, how do you feel about it these days?"

"You mean, do I really want to win?" She nodded, and he continued. "Some days yes, some days no. I think I could be a pretty good president, but I have to admit your ideas for change and serious improvements in student government are awfully strong. And it's true that Sally is going all out on catchy advertising techniques.

Now I may make up points in my platform speech, but well. . . ." His voice trailed off, and he brought his head down close to hers. "But if I had to make a choice, I'd say my first priority wasn't the election. It's—"

They were rudely interrupted when the door banged open behind them, nearly knocking them both sideways off the step.

"What the—? Hey, I didn't see you guys!" Spike Turner was standing above them, holding a full glass of soda. Luckily, he jerked his hand just before it poured all over Steve, and the soda hit the rosebushes instead. "Boy, super party, Carole! You sure know how to fix 'em." He sighed, easing his considerable bulk down next to Steve, who inched even closer to Carole. She thought that this sort of made up for the fact that he had swiftly removed his arm from around her shoulder the instant Spike had appeared.

"Glad you're having fun." Carole smiled politely, wishing Spike had had a little better timing.

"Yeah, well, Sally's really yakking it up in there," he went on, not realizing that he'd disturbed anything. "She's got one terrific following, I'll say that." He looked terribly disgruntled, and Carole suddenly felt sorry for him. "Have to admit," he went on, "my marks have sort of suffered since I started this campaigning business. It'll be good to get back to normal, right?"

He turned to them for support, but all he got were two puzzled looks.

"I can't speak for Carole," Steve said, "but I haven't given up."

"Me either," she chimed in hotly. "Come on, Steve. Let's go investigate this brilliant third party and her gang." She got up and dusted off the back of her dress. "Spike," she threw over her shoulder, "one thing that makes a candidate survive is stick-to-itiveness." She didn't catch Steve's proud smile as she walked into the kitchen, but he was right behind her—in more ways than one.

"And therefore"—Sally's high-pitched voice carried all the way across the living room and into the kitchen—"there's no reason why our class can't have the best prom ever, for the least amount of money. You know that that old band the seniors always hire is from the Dark Ages. My father has this great group playing at his restaurant right now, and they'd be delighted to perform for old Twain High."

"A pro band—wow!" Irv Bates exclaimed.

"Sally, if you'd give another candidate a chance, *I'd* like to talk." Michael pushed his way across the room.

Carole gave Steve a disgusted look and hurried into the living room. What nerve these people had, to do their campaigning in another candidate's house!

"What about the yearbook, Sally?" asked Eleanor Laiken. "Don't you have some ideas about that?"

Carole sighed and shifted her weight uncomfortably. "That question is a plant if I ever saw one," she muttered to Steve under her breath. "Eleanor's her best friend—she knows her platform better than her own name. This really burns me up."

For a minute she just wanted to throw Sally out. Then she wondered if she should start making a speech herself on the other side of the room, and see if she could attract a crowd. But as she was debating with herself, Steve came to the rescue.

"That's very interesting, Sally," he cut in. "Why don't we continue this on Tuesday in the platform assembly?" Steve, the perfect charmer as always, guided Sally swiftly away from her little group and nearly dragged her into the kitchen to fill up her plate. When they went through the swinging door, Sally was jabbering happily to him, scarcely upset that her plot to take over the evening had been foiled.

"That was neat." Carole turned around to see Dave standing behind her, his arms folded across his skinny chest. "Did you see how he did that? Your boyfriend has *real* smarts."

"He isn't my boyfriend." Carole spoke clearly and distinctly.

But if that were true, why was it that when everyone left about two hours later, she felt so sad to see Steve go? And why was she sorry not to have that little crick in her neck that she always used to have after he kissed her good night?

Trying not to think about it, she began what was sure to be a very long cleanup.

Chapter Nine

Carole had promised to meet Mary Ann at G. Fox as soon as school let out, to shop for her assembly clothes, but her mind was elsewhere as she pedaled her bike out of Twain High's parking lot on her way to the center of town. The only thing she could think about was Steve at the party on Saturday night. The hazy moon, the sweet smells of spring, the sensation of his large, warm hand on her shoulder. It was a terrible mistake to be thinking this way—she knew it! It was counterproductive and demoralizing, not to mention hopeless. What if he'd just been in a mood that night? What if it was just his own nervousness about winning that made him put his arm around her?

And the worst was still to come. Steve Landy was sure to win the last round of the election—the speeches at the platform assembly. She was well aware that he could talk circles around her and could probably demolish Sally, Connie, Spike, and Pete, too, with a flick of his *Robert's Rules of Order.* Michael would probably give a smooth speech, except somehow his words never stuck after the neatness of his performance was over. And she felt bad for Bobby, since he had some good ideas that would be lost in his nervous delivery.

Steve was such a determined fighter, she knew he was going to try his very best. Naturally, she would, too. She was counting on her summation speech to turn the tide toward her. She was a lousy debater, but she did have ideas, and she hoped she could make up for her limitations with a rock-em-sock-em speech.

"Well, it's about time!" Mary Ann greeted her at the bike stand beside the department store. "I've been waiting twenty minutes."

Carole locked her bicycle and glanced at her watch. "I was talking to Dave. He's publishing the polls this afternoon, and I wanted to get an early look at who's ahead." She raised her hands when her friend looked at her questioningly. "The trend is that there's no trend. Everyone's about equal. C'mon, let's get me some clothes," she said, pulling Mary Ann through the front doorway.

"I think whatever you wear should be simple and tasteful," Mary Ann said, as they rode the escalator up to the junior department.

"And cheap. My allowance has somehow vanished into thin air this month. I'm getting a job this summer," Carole declared to a mannequin at the top of the escalator. "I'm going to be totally independent."

"Oh, yeah," Mary Ann scoffed, making a direct line toward the sportswear.

"You don't understand," Carole said, stopping her friend before she could throw an awful floral print smock dress at her. "That's not me," she said emphatically. "Hey, I never went with the crowd or compromised my principles before the election, and you should understand that I'm not going to start now! But I really think, whether I win some office or not, I've gotten something invaluable out of this."

"Yeah, Steve does sort of seem interested in you again, come to think of it," Mary Ann said grinning.

"*Mary Ann!* That's not what I meant at all." Carole's eyes snapped with a bright, clear energy. "Don't you see? It's all coming together. The election, Plant Life sounding good, writing my own interview, speaking in public. It's like I've become more alive or something." She waved away another awful dress and shook a warning finger at her friend. "Now, listen. I tried your way of dressing for the party. But it didn't do anything to help me as far as I can see. The point of clothing is that it should suit the wearer." She nodded emphatically as she strolled to the next rack. "Like this outfit is me."

It consisted of a pair of white peg pants that came to just above the ankle and a green, square-necked cotton top that buttoned diagonally across the front.

"I'd wear it with white knee-highs and my red sneakers. And I'd feel comfortable."

Mary Ann covered her face with her hands and groaned. "Suicide. I didn't realize you were bent on self-destruction."

"MA, I'm the liberal candidate, for Pete's sake. I can't come on dressed like somebody's mother."

"Yeah, but one of the Three Stooges isn't such a hot image, either."

Carole took a size five off the rack and marched purposefully to the dressing room to try on the outfit. The checker gave her a ticket and directed her to a cubicle, and Mary Ann trailed behind, basically resigned to her friend's bad judgment in clothes.

"What do you think Steve's going to wear?" she asked, watching Carole tear out of her jeans and plaid shirt.

"Guys have it easy. It's just slacks and a jacket, and they're ready to go."

"He looked pretty cool the other night, don't you think?" Mary Ann asked casually. "Mmm," Carole said noncommittally as she pulled on the pants.

"Hey, that's not as bad as I thought it was going to be," Mary Ann said, when Carole had the new outfit on.

"You are what you wear—you know the old saying," Carole said, regarding herself in the three-way mirror. "OK, this is it." She glanced at the price tag and started to change back into her old clothes. "I've turned over a new leaf, Mary Ann. It's independence all the way. If you're true to yourself, no matter what people think about your personal style, they've got to respect you."

Slinging her new outfit defiantly over one arm, she stalked out of the dressing room and went directly to the cashier's desk.

"Do me a favor," Mary Ann said quietly behind her, while Carole fumbled for her wallet. "Wear whatever you want, campaign however you want, but please, don't get up in that assembly and preach. Carole, this is only a high-school election, you know. Kids don't want a lot of seriousness and high pressure."

"Um," Carole responded a bit shortly, watching the cashier pack up her new purchases. "You leave it to me—I know what the people want, MA, really I do."

They strolled through the store in silence, neither of them feeling awfully friendly. Carole knew that Mary Ann had done a lot to help her with this election, but now she was on her own, and that was sort of scary, although very exhilarating. Dave's advice had taken her part of the way, as had Mary Ann's prodding and Steve's interest. But now nothing was left but

149

the last lonely mile to the finish line. If she wanted the job, if she really cared more about winning than about anything else, she could do it. She was positive that it was all a question of attitude and of priorities. The thing was, right now she just didn't know whether the greatest victory meant winning or losing the election. Oddly enough, she wasn't as afraid of failure as she was of the thought that success might drive her and Steve apart—just when they were getting close. Unless, of course, her dream that they would both be elected came true. But that was too much to count on.

She liked Steve so much, but she liked herself, too. With such split loyalties, how was she ever going to fight as hard as she ought to?

The next morning dawned sunny and cool. Carole took a shortcut to school and went directly to her favorite spot, a tucked-away patch of grass in back of the gym. Squinting up at the morning sunlight, she sat down, cross-legged, on her bookbag, so as to avoid grass stains on her new white pants, and concentrated on relaxing. This was a technique she'd been trying for weeks without much success, but maybe, with her summation speech only a scant hour away, it might work for her. She began to mutter.

"Big toe—relax! Kneecap—relax! Come on arms, let go!" She repeated these sentences about wenty-five times in succession, until they didn't nean very much at all. You were supposed to go through all the parts of your body and command them to calm down. Then you were supposed to feel better all over. But hard as she tried, the weird feeling in the bottom of her lungs that made breathing difficult refused to vanish.

"Yuck!" she said at last, getting up with a disgusted snort. "Relaxing is for the birds." Some small part of her was holding back, she knew. As much as she vowed she was an independent spirit, free of peer pressure, parental demands, and self-doubts, she still felt tied up in knots.

The front hall was filling up with members of the junior class. Everybody grinned at her and smiled idiotically. Today she was a celebrity and not because she was in a rock band. She was poised on the pinnacle of stardom, and one false move could push her off the edge.

"If the candidates will please step into Dr. Larkin's office," boomed a voice over the loudspeaker, "he would like a brief word with you before the election assembly begins."

A path opened up in the milling crowd for Carole, and, as though in a daze, she walked through the lined-up kids. She could see Sally deep in conversation with Irv Bates right in front of Dr. Larkin's door.

"Are you all right?" A voice beside her made her jump.

"Oh! Hi, MA, sorry." Carole rubbed her hands together nervously. They were damp and clammy. "Just fogging out."

"Yeah, well, don't fog out in the assembly." Mary Ann looked carefully at Carole's face. "Did you eat breakfast? You're not feeling faint, are you?" She hovered over Carole like a mother hen.

"I'm fine," Carole said, laughing. "Everything's fine," she insisted, repeating the words as though they were true.

"Well, go on, will you? Time's running out." Mary Ann pushed her to the door.

"Don't I know it?" She walked stolidly forward into the lion's den.

Steve was already waiting inside, and Sally was standing close to Dr. Larkin's desk. All the other candidates shuffled in after Carole.

"Aw right, young ladies and gentlemen." The jovial principal beamed. "Just wanted to tell y'all what a fine election you've run so far and to express my sincere enthusiasm and interest."

There was a long, awkward silence while everyone waited for Dr. Larkin to say something profound, but he just kept smiling at each of them and nodding his head. Carole's throat felt all gluey, and she feared there wouldn't be enough saliva left in her mouth to get her through her speech. If only Dr. Larkin would keep them all in his office for a long pep talk. Naturally, that was too much to hope for. After walking to each candidate and shaking his or her hand, the principal nodded once more and gestured at the door.

"It's about that time now, I guess. So let's go on and talk up a storm. Remember, this is your last chance to get votes."

Carole filed out behind the other candidates and followed Dr. Larkin down the corridor to the backstage entrance of the auditorium. She was simply astounded that her feet kept moving, taking one firm step after the other. The last thing she was conscious of as the heavy stage door closed behind her was Steve's hand clutching hers. And she was relieved to see, when she looked up into his face, that he was as nervous as she was!

Chapter Ten

Carole walked onstage in a haze. She was vaguely aware of eight chairs and one center seat behind a lectern, which was for the moderator of the assembly. Dave had been asked to take that job, but in his usual disregard for "establishment games," as he called them, he'd bowed out. Max Schoen, Steve's best friend, was the next logical choice, since he was the Twain *Herald*'s political reporter.

Carole looked out to see the auditorium filling up. Aside from the day she had accepted the nomination, which she had basically botched by falling flat on her face on the stage, she had never stood up and talked in front of this many people. How many were hostile? she wondered, scanning the faces. How many solidly for her? How many did she still have a chance of convincing?

She glanced over at Steve, who seemed miles

away on the large stage. It was true—he was her most worthy adversary, just as she was his. The two of them had the most casual and easy styles of all the candidates, but it was difficult to say what their chances were against Sally.

Carole shifted her gaze to the prim, blond, rapidly blinking candidate. *She must be nervous*—she *has* to be. But Sally's placid face betrayed not a shred of doubt. She was perched on her chair like a bird about to take flight, careful not to muss the back of her skirt.

The house lights dimmed in the auditorium, and the stage lights came up a notch, hitting Carole right in the face. The only good thing about that was that she couldn't see the faces of her listeners. It all looked like a blank wall of noses and hair, which was fine with her.

Max Schoen pushed his tortoiseshell glasses up on the bridge of his nose and walked to the front of the stage. He was a serious guy, who was predictable and very loyal. He and Steve had been friends since fifth grade, and Carole realized it must be hard for him not to take sides. His neatly combed red hair lay flat, and his shoes had been shined to brilliant perfection.

"Dr. Larkin, members of the faculty, fellow students, and candidates," he began. "I will state the rules of this discussion, and then we'll begin. Each candidate will present his or her platform speech. Then I will take questions from the audience, each of which should be directed at a specific candidate. These questions should deal with the material covered in the speeches. All right. . . ." He raised his hands like a ringmaster about to start the circus. "Our first candidate for president of the senior class, Pete Kelly."

Carole faded in and out of Pete's speech. He had a piece of paper in front of him with a lot of figures on it, but it didn't help him to be any clearer in his thinking. The only thing on Carole's mind was that she was last. They had all drawn numbers for the speaking order, and she had pulled number eight. By the time her turn came, she worried, the kids in the audience would either be wriggling in their seats or have firmly decided on their preferred candidate. Why did she have such luck? she agonized, as Pete droned on.

There was a smattering of applause as Pete finished speaking and took his seat, looking enormously relieved that it was all over with. Max got up again and introduced Connie, and Carole forced herself to listen to this one. She'd been right—Connie's heart wasn't in it. The next speaker was Michael, who started off strong, but he tossed in every campaign promise he could think of and made his speech far too long. Then there was Bobby, who, as predicted, was so scared he could hardly project into the microphone.

At last Max introduced Steve, his voice ringing with pride and clear bias in favor of his friend. The fifth candidate took his place at the podium in front of the microphone, and Carole couldn't help thinking that he sure would make a cute president.

Stop thinking this way! she yelled silently at herself.

"Good morning." Steve's voice was mellow, betraying none of the nervousness that Carole knew was there. This election really did mean a lot to him, she mused. It wasn't just winning, it was doing the job right. Did she feel as committed as he was? She sank deeper into her chair and listened.

"I know you've all been waiting for this week, but not as much as I have."

A ripple of laughter passed through the huge room, and Steve looked pleased that he'd gotten the desired reaction.

"A school election is an important thing. But not for the candidates—not for the eight of us up here. It's important for *you*, because the outcome means a decision about what kind of government you're going to have for the next year. Now I could stand here and talk about all my promises—the reserved spaces for seniors with stickers in the parking lot, the fund-raisers, the student-faculty discussion groups to air differences and come up with answers to tough problems. But you've read all that in the *Herald*, in my interview. As a matter of fact, you've read about all of us already. And you know we're all genuine in our concern for Twain High, otherwise we wouldn't have been busting our chops for the past four weeks, or stuck it out."

More laughter, very appreciative this time, Carole felt. Steve raised his hands for silence in a very professional manner, and only when the big room was quiet, did he speak into the microphone again. "OK, so you know all that. So what else is new? I decided to get up here today and tell you about elections in general—not my election in particular. I want this class to have an excellent group of officers, sure, because we all do, and it's got to be a group that works together, without petty jealousies or self-serving goals. I guess the hardest thing for us to grasp is that however you decide to vote on Friday, your participation in this election is the most important thing. It will prepare you for the time when you'll have a say in the political process of our country. This is more than campaign promises or senior activities." He leaned forward, scanning the whole room. "This is real life, guys." He nodded. "This is the democratic process at work."

The applause broke out at once, enthusiastic and deafening. Carole sat quietly, as did the other candidates, but she couldn't help thinking that Steve's delivery and rah-rah energy sounded better than the actual content of his speech. This was pretty inflated stuff to throw at high-school kids, for heaven's sake. She had wanted to like his speech, but she found it lacking in something. His grandiose comparisons to the world at large turned her right off. She tried to look at him critically, not nastily, but with a keen eye to his qualifications. Cute president or no, boyfriend or adversary, it didn't matter. If she was just another kid, she wouldn't vote for him, not on the basis of that speech, anyway.

"Thank you very much, Steve Landy," Max said as the applause died down. "Our next speaker will be Sally Scott."

Then something funny happened. As Carole watched Sally take her place in front of the mike, a rustle started in the auditorium. She could just barely make out activity way in the back. But something else was going on, over on the left side. What was this? Signs on placards appeared in the two areas. Some people were even wearing hats, advertising their candidate! The Sally Scott caucus had plastered the house. Across the stage, Carole could see Steve fuming. What a dirty trick! Suddenly his words came back to her—self-serving goals, indeed!

Sally nodded graciously to her supporters and then stuck her mouth up close to the mike. "Hi," she breathed. She paused slightly and then continued. "I'd just like to start out by thanking everyone—the faculty, the administration, and all of *you*"—she stressed the last word—"for the great help and support you've given me over the past few weeks. I assure you that if elected, I'm going to return the favor many times over. I've given a lot of thought to being senior class president, and it's often occurred to me that holding such a position is more a responsibility than an honor. I owe it to you, my fellow students, to give you the most. I owe you more than I can ever say, but I'll start out with just a few items."

She was interrupted by applause from her claque. Carole peered out, wondering how many of these dodos there really were, and if there were enough to hurt her chances.

"OK, now, I want to mention a topic of interest to all of you. The senior prom."

Carole rolled her eyes to the ceiling. She could just imagine Dave's running commentary to *this* speech.

"I think I can pretty well guarantee the best prom Twain High has ever seen. A great band, a catered meal, and the best time you ever had in your life—all at the Beresford House."

Carole's heart sank. The Beresford House was Sally's father's beautiful, posh restaurant. She would have no trouble at all arranging to have the place closed for a night. What other candidate could deliver that kind of goods? If, that is, the senior prom was the most urgent issue on every junior's mind.

Carole looked over and caught a glimpse of the disgusted expression on Steve's face. He evidently didn't appreciate Sally's tactics any more than she did. But oddly enough, this nonsense of Sally's just stimulated Carole. It goaded her on to make the best possible speech with the finest possible delivery.

Sally continued. "I think that the senior classes in years past have made the mistake of trying too hard to be socially conscious. I mean, it goes without saying that we all *care*. . . ." Sally looked out at the crowd with a serious expression. "But it also seems clear that we are kids, and we've got plenty of years ahead of us when there won't be time for fun and games. So what am I saying, really? I'm saying I want to be president, and I want to do what's right for all of you." She stretched out her arms, embracing the whole notion of power and privilege. The room burst into cheers and applause.

The odd thing about all this, Carole mused, was Sally's inconsistency. In her interview in the *Herald*, she had been full of plans and programs and committees. In the meeting with the faculty, she had bent over backward to please the teachers. And now, in front of her public, she was Miss Good Time Charlene. It was confusing, to say the least. Carole just prayed that Sally's rather scattered image would work against her. And against the squawking throng who was working for her.

"And in conclusion," Sally said, dropping her voice to a syrup-smooth slither, "I simply have to say this: If you elect me senior class president, I will see to it that all of you are rewarded with the most fantastic year of your life. Thank you."

The applause that began almost before she had finished made the reaction to Steve's speech look like a paltry joke. And, unfortunately, it wasn't only Sally's gang thumping their feet. A lot of kids who hadn't cared about the election before were now hooked on Sally's promises.

Smiling and waving as she backed up toward her seat, Sally kept the noise going in the auditorium for a good three minutes. To Carole, it seemed like an eternity before Max got up again and shuffled over to the mike. "Our next candidate, Spike Turner."

Poor Spike. He looked so uncomfortable as he approached the mike. Outclassed and lacking any oomph to carry his speech across, he looked like a large, lost puppy. Sally was a hard act to follow in any case, but what could he say to grab the crowd's attention? He cleared his throat for about the twentieth time and began.

"I am . . . *Aaargh!*" He licked his lips and stuck two fingers in his neck band, trying to ease the pressure of the stiffly starched collar his mother had clearly insisted he wear. "Yeah, ah . . . *harumph*. Um, I'd like to be elected president . . . because I'm the kind of guy you can talk to. You know, I won't be kind of removed or distant or. . . . I'm a regular guy, and

I think Twain needs a regular guy. I mean . . .
it's hard to say whether anyone can make good
on campaign promises, so all you know for sure
is what you got right in front of you. . . . *Ah-
hem.* OK, so I think you ought to elect me
because there'd be no surprises. Everything,
ah, OK." Spike took a deep breath.

"That's about it," he muttered. "Unaccustomed
as I am to public speaking, I'll stop right here."
He took a silly little bow and retreated hastily to
his seat. There was a smattering of applause
that stopped as abruptly as his speech had.

Max Schoen approached the dais again. "Our
last candidate, Carole Weiss."

Here it comes, go on and slay 'em. Carole
wiped her hands on her pant legs one final
time, steeling herself. She felt awfully sorry for
Spike, but there was nothing she could do to
show him she was sympathetic. Now was the
moment to put aside all thoughts except that of
the one shining goal that could be—might be—
hers with a bit of effort. She was going to talk
as she never had before.

She had prepared well for this event. Taking
her place in front of the mike, she spent a
couple of moments lowering it to her height.
She was shorter than any of the other candidates, so naturally it was way too high for
her. Instead of standing in front of it like a
statue for her whole speech, she intended to
remove the mike from its stand and work the

house, just like the rock musician she was. But for now, she stood quietly, gathering energy. When everyone was silent, she spoke.

"My fellow candidates have covered a lot of territory here today, and I'm sure that something each of them said has struck a note within you. There are all kinds of ways to approach the leadership of Twain High's senior class—probably as many ways as there are people in this whole auditorium."

She could sense Steve's eyes boring holes into her back and decided that whether he was feeling positive or negative about her right now, she would use his interest to her own advantage. She quickly unclipped the mike and walked to the apron of the stage.

"Why do we need leaders in high school? I mean, there are still higher powers, right? There's the school administration and our teachers and our parents, and they all make rules we have to follow, a kind of minigovernment, if you want to look at it that way. Then you have your city government and the state of Connecticut and the fed." She turned to her fellow candidates to include them and honed right in on Steve. "Boy, that's a lot of rules to follow!"

The laughter was low and warm, and she caught a glimpse of what victory could mean. She flipped the mike cord behind her and strolled along the stage.

"Now with all that, what can student government mean? Why do you want it?" She whirled around to face the house and pointed at the students dramatically. "Because it's your own because you made it. And for me to be your president, or any of the other candidates," she went on, "will mean a vote for your own independence and self-respect. That means you have to choose carefully when you vote on Friday."

She moved back along the apron, never turning her back to the audience. "Now I'm not going to build castles in the air, OK? Sure, I talked about a senior lounge and a class trip. I'd like to do a lot of things, including stuff like proms and yearbooks and dances as well as the serious things. The elementary school lunch program, for example, is urgent right now, at a time when a lot of little kids are getting dumped on because of budgetary cutbacks. See, governments can do a lot of harm and a lot of good at the same time. And, folks, if elected"—Carole eased her way back to the podium and snapped the mike in place—"I'm going to see to it that you all get a say in this. I'd lead, but I wouldn't want you to follow blindly. It's up to all of us to make this work."

Her voice rang with passion and enthusiasm. It wasn't until she'd actually stood up there in front of an audience and blasted out her ideas in front of hundreds of people that she realized what a good job she really could do if given the opportunity. She might be a flake, as Mary Ann said, but she had principles.

"And the main thing is this," she concluded, her dark eyes flashing around the big hall. "Everybody get out there on Friday and vote for one of us. Just do it, because not only is that how you make the system work—that's how, if you want to, you can change the system. Thank you."

She stood poised on the balls of her feet, waiting. She counted one, two, three—no applause! Absolute silence. She wanted to die; she'd bombed. Then, when she could stand it no longer, on the count of four, the noise began. It wasn't as wild and abundant as the applause for Sally, but it was easily as good as that for Steve. With a sigh of relief, and a taste of metal in her dry mouth, she went back to her seat and tried not to collapse into it.

As Max walked back to the podium, there was a lot of rustling, people chattering to their neighbors, adjusting positions, and scribbling questions on the note pads that they had all been told to bring to the assembly.

The house lights snapped on, and Max called for the first question. Carole wasn't too surprised when it was directed at Sally. Then there were a few for Steve—all from girls, Carole noted suspiciously—and more for Sally. Michael and Connie fielded about three each; Bobby none at all. One really awful moment came when somebody from the back asked Spike whom he liked for the World Series, which caused the whole hall to crack up. Carole answered a few directed at her, but she wasn't thinking on her feet, and she thought her responses were pretty naive.

Finally the bell rang for the end of the period, and Max quickly drew the program to a close. Carole was limp in her seat—every bone in her body had turned to jelly.

"I'd like to thank the candidates," Max intoned, "and to congratulate them all on a job well done. And as for the rest of you"—he looked out at the students in the audience, who were all gathering their books for the next class—"I hope to see you at the polls. They open at eight Friday morning and will close promptly at two so that the tallying can begin. In the case of a tie, there will be a runoff ballot Monday morning. That's about it except—" He turned back to the candidates. "May the best person win!"

As Carole filed offstage with the others, she felt a mixture of excitement and relief. She had fought the good fight, and now there was nothing to do but wait. Friday was only about a hundred light years away.

Chapter Eleven

Carole went through the rest of the day in a fog. Lots of people came up to congratulate her and tell her how impressed they were with her speech, but others—some kids she'd been really friendly with—pointedly avoided her. They gave her that creepy "I don't have to smile at you" fish-eye stare. Minds were being made up all over Twain High.

When the last bell of the day rang, she wandered glumly down to her locker to get her guitar. She had a rehearsal of Plant Life, although she couldn't imagine how she was going to be able to concentrate on anything but the election until Friday.

When she arrived at the Brunos' house half an hour later, the girls were just setting up. Mary Ann thumped her on the back and said she was a great public speaker; Ellen was a little too enthusiastic, giving Carole the sinking

169

feeling she'd made up her mind to vote for some-body else. But who? Sally? Steve? After all, she had seconded Carole's nomination. Would Ellen really vote for Steve? Thinking about this made her wonder about all those girls in the question-and-answer period who'd been so interested in Steve.

I'm a mess, Carole thought, as she began tuning up. *How could I ever be president of the senior class with an attitude like this?*

It was true that ever since she had gotten all enthused about doing her own thing and get-ting elected, a lot of weird things had happened to her. She couldn't concentrate on the right stuff at the right time, and what was worse, now she was jealous because of Steve! Carole Weiss, poisoned by ugly, nasty jealousy. It was unthinkable. Even when she had been going out with Steve, she had never acted jealous if he looked at another girl. But then, he never had, she recalled. He'd been simply crazy about her, as a matter of fact. Why should she be jealous now?

"Well, are you going to stare into space, or are you going to listen to the downbeat?" Janice was glaring at Carole, and the other girls looked pretty impatient, too.

"Sorry, it's only . . . I've got a lot on my mind," Carole murmured, wishing that everybody would stop what they were doing and just take a min-ute to listen to her. Here she was, running for the highest office in the school, and suddenly she felt more vulnerable than she ever had in her life. Not that she wasn't competent and independent and everything, but she was something else, too. Everybody had always thought of wise-cracking Carole as tough and funny and wrapped in her own layer of Styrofoam so that she was virtually unbreakable. But she had changed over the course of one month. All the competition, all the public notice, had made her look inside and take a peek at the Carole lurking in the depths. She didn't have to have her own way all the time, and she could allow her parents or teachers or grown-ups in general to have their say, too. Even Steve.

Well, of course, you dummy, she thought, with a burst of understanding. You didn't like him because he acted like a grown-up, and all you wanted to be was a bratty little kid. Suddenly she wanted to fly out of Janice's basement and go talk to Steve. But she couldn't do that. She had a responsibility to her group, and suddenly, feeling very mature, she told herself how important it was to stick to her commitments and stand by the people who really mattered to her. Carole picked up her guitar and started to play.

"Ellen, you never come in fast enough at the break," Mary Ann complained, after they'd done their opening number a couple of times.

"I'm pausing," she said, tossing her blond mane over one shoulder.

"Well, pause faster!" Alice urged her, hitting the cymbal to start up again. "C'mon, Carole. A-one, a-two, a-one, two, three. . . ."

Carole strummed for all she was worth and managed to catch the complicated rhythm of the next number right on cue. The girls were sweating and exhausted after forty minutes of playing.

"Ellen, can you use the mike the way Carole did today in the assembly?" MA asked, when they took their first break. "It's really effective," she added, with a smile to Carole. "*You* were really effective."

"Oh, thanks," Carole said, taking a seat beside Ellen. "Nothing to it," she explained to the singer.

"I'm afraid I'll trip over the cord if I move around that much," Ellen wailed.

"You saw what Carole did when she was walking around. She just swung it out of the way and kept moving. Use both hands and your whole body. Be involved!" Mary Ann insisted.

"Hey, I'm a singer, not a politician," Ellen muttered.

"Oh, for heaven's sake," Alice grumbled. "That's not the point."

"Yeah," Carole said, grinning. "Maybe I'm more of a rock musician than a politician. It's just technique, Ellen," she encouraged her. "A little

172

razzle-dazzle gets 'em every time. That's the whole secret of performing in public, I've learned. You don't have to be that good. All you gotta do is hold their attention."

"Hmmm," Ellen murmured, considering the idea. "I see what you mean. Well, I'll try it. Will you help me, Carole?" she asked.

"I'd love to." Carole was secretly thrilled to have an assignment like this. It was usually easier to forget her own problems when she dug into somebody else's. "OK, Plant Life," she said, getting to her feet again. "Let's *grow* a little!"

Giggling and laughing, spurred on by new enthusiasm and teamwork, the girls started up again. And when they were finished, Mrs. Bruno stuck her head through the doorway and exclaimed, "That sounded good!"

As soon as dinner was over, Carole went upstairs to her room to call Dave. He was her best critic, and he never failed to pick out her strongest and weakest points. She thought about calling Steve, but she was nervous about what he'd think. There was nothing wrong with phoning, of course, but their status as competitors made things awkward. She sat on the edge of her bed and nervously fiddled with the phone cord. Then, at last, she dialed.

"Hi. How's it going?" she asked Dave as soon

as he picked up. "You got a minute to talk about you know what?"

"The speech, you mean? It was OK."

Carole sighed. "Don't humor me. Give it to me straight."

"No, hey, I just did. But as I see it, it won't make a lot of difference one way or another. Pete never was in the running for president, and I don't think Twain High's sports fans are a strong enough constituency to get Spike into office. Bobby? He doesn't have what it takes. I like him, but forget it. OK, Connie has half a chance, but Michael might be able to swing it—at least I think he could. But you and Landy and Scott were always neck and neck for the lead, and you still are."

"Do you really think I have a chance?" she asked him.

"Well, if I voted, and I don't think I will, I'd vote for you. For your principles, understand. But you do have some stiff competition, and there's a lot of difference in your platforms."

"I know what you mean."

"Yeah, well first you have Sally Scott, the creep-o candidate. She'd buy her way into office quicker than I can say horsefeathers. But the crowd is greedy, right? They want to know what you've done for them lately. So she could sway them." He gave a disgusted hoot.

"Yes," prompted Carole, really interested. "Next?"

"Next you got Landy, the charmer. He's tall, he's got a chiseled jaw, OK? He's like a Kennedy. Now that's gonna cause some little female hearts to start fluttering."

Carole sat up so suddenly, she hit her head on the shelf above her bed. "What do you mean?"

"You know. All the oohs and ahs he gets when he talks. Makes me sick," Dave declared. "And then we move on to you. Now your only problem, as I see it, is you come on like some kind of free spirit. In the stratosphere."

"What!" Carole shrieked. "That's an awful thing to say. And it's not true."

"Carole, hold on. I mean it as a compliment. I think it's nice that you're for the people—less aristocracy, more group rule. You'll attract the bleeding-heart liberals like me, who believe that there's life after the prom. I don't know how many of us there are, though," he added glumly. "You have to look at this realistically."

"I'm trying," she told him.

"Just cool it, would you?" he went on. "I mean, it's all pretty silly, isn't it?"

"How can you say that?" Carole demanded. "You're the one who just outlined all the differences in the candidates for me. That means there's a choice. And as long as the electorate has a choice, it's their duty to pick one."

"Boy! You sure sound like a politician now, kid! Well, I tell you what. Seeing as how you're so excited about this, maybe I'll vote after all. It won't mean much, but I may just do it anyhow."

"Cynic," Carole accused him. "Well, sleep on it, and see how you feel in the morning, will you?"

"For you," he agreed, "anything. Catch you later."

"Bye, Dave." She hung up, terribly confused. How persuasive was she, really? Maybe Dave was only humoring her and didn't intend to vote at all.

But then she wondered, did all this really make the difference she kept insisting it did? Was there an actual choice? Were there leaders and followers in her senior class, just as there were in America as a whole? In the tiny microcosm of Twain High, not caring seemed to be the worst problem. If a smart guy like Dave could shrug and walk away from the polls, what were all the other students doing? Was this election really just a popularity contest, where the "best" was ignored and the prize was meaningless?

Feeling exhausted, Carole got ready for bed and turned out the lights without even saying good night to her parents. It all looked pretty hopeless right now— whether she got elected or not. She climbed into bed and fell into an uneasy sleep, rocked by dreams and the phantoms of her overactive imagination.

*   *   *

Anyone who overheard the conversations in the halls of Twain High during the next few days knew that many students had already reached a decision. The weeks of campaigning were about over, the speeches and interviews given, and it was almost time to find out just how effective the gimmicks and platforms of the candidates had been. Voting was on every junior's mind, although nobody talked much about it. On Thursday, the election committee got to work setting up the auditorium like a polling place, and that was when Carole's stomach started doing somersaults. The only thing that kept her sane was the thought that Mary Ann was coming over with some new albums to take her mind off the ordeal.

"I got away as soon as I could," Mary Ann said when Carole opened the door for her after supper. "My mom's very sympathetic, by the way," she added. "And she says she really hopes you win."

"Thanks," Carole murmured, leading her friend through the living room to the hall stairs and starting to climb.

"How're you feeling?" Mary Ann scrutinized Carole's rather white face. "You look awful."

"Kind of you to say so," Carole said as they entered the bedroom. "Wow, where'd you get all these?" she exclaimed, as Mary Ann opened the large tote bag she was carrying and started pulling out album after album.

"Oh, you know. They just multiply, like rab-
bits. You go past the music store, and it's hard
to pass up the latest release." She began arranging an order. "A slow one first," Mary Ann
said, picking a soft, jazz-funk group. "You need
to calm down."

"Thanks," Carole nodded, gratefully letting
Mary Ann take charge. "I guess you're right.
Boy, I wish the election was over."

"Soon enough," said wise old Mary Ann. "Now
tell me, you don't really expect to win, do you?
Just between you and me."

"Well," Carole pondered, "Dave says I have a
chance according to preliminary polls. But I
guess, to be perfectly honest, I think it's a toss-
up between Steve and Sally for the presidency."

"Now what about him?" Mary Ann asked.

"What about him?"

"Don't play dumb, Carole. I saw you two at
the party, all starry-eyed. I've never seen you
like that."

"Big expert on me, aren't you?" Carole asked,
secretly admitting that Mary Ann was right.
She'd been thinking about Steve nonstop for a
couple of weeks now. No wonder it showed!

"Well, what are you going to do if he's elected
president?"

"I'll congratulate him, naturally. I'll even hand
him a couple of my ideas if he gives me proper
credit and lets me put them into motion," she
said staunchly. Then her resolve crumpled, and

178

she made a face. "Truth is, though," she said softly, "I'll be enormously depressed. I mean, he'll be on top, and I'll be just another presidential hanger-on. He'll have so many committee meetings and faculty-student things to organize, not to mention functions like dances and fundraisers, that I'll never get to see him."

"Don't underestimate yourself," Mary Ann said, and grinned. "When you want to do something, you do it. Remember, there's always the possibility that you'll be elected to another position. Anyhow, I have a feeling that one way or the other, he might just ask you out."

"Fat chance," Carole grumbled. "He said he was going to ask me out weeks ago when we had a Coke together."

Mary Ann looked up, astonished. "You never told me about that. I thought this whole avoidance thing was going to last till the election and then, boom! You'd fall into each other's arms."

Carole sighed at her friend's optimism. "Sounds nice, doesn't it? But if I win, he might never speak to me again."

"Don't be too sure. Some men really admire women in power. Besides, will you be angry with him if he wins?"

"No, of course not. But Steve, well, I can see he's changed a lot in the past year, but I'd just assume that he wouldn't be thrilled about me winning." The phone rang, but Carole ignored it. Her mother would pick up—she always did.

She watched MA flip the records. "Wonder what he's doing right now?" Carole murmured.

"Worrying, like you. I think, personally, that the political race has been a good test for both of you. I mean, if you can compete like crazy with a guy and still be silly in love the way you are. . . ." She let the sentence hang in the air.

"Who said anything about love?" Carole asked hotly. "I'm not in love, for heaven's sake."

There was a knock at the door, and Mrs. Weiss stuck her head in. "Phone call for you, sweetie." She smiled at her daughter. "It's Steve Landy."

"Oh, no!" Carole wailed.

Mary Ann stood up and did a little jig. "I knew it!" she crowed. "Well, I'll get lost for a while."

Carole sat there resignedly, and Mary Ann went downstairs to the den. The phone receiver lay on its cradle and just before she picked it up, she pictured Steve on the other end of the line, his cheek resting against the phone, just as she would like it to be resting against hers.

"Hello?" she heard her mother hang up.

"Hi!" he said, his voice low and teasing. "Just wanted to see how you were doing. I'm climbing walls over here," he confessed.

"Yeah, me too. Mary Ann came over to help me through it."

"I'm glad you're in the same shape I am," he

told her. "It's a real lonely feeling, like you're the only person in the world."

"But you've run for other offices before," Carole pointed out.

"This is different, though," he told her. "Look, whoever wins tomorrow, I just want you to know I wish you luck. You've done a terrific job on this campaign. And no hard feelings, OK?"

"Of course not," she said decisively, hoping that he was about to say something personal.

"I think you'd make a fine president, Carole."

"You, too," she muttered. *Get to the point, will you, Landy?*

But he didn't say anything else, and all she could hear was his breathing on the other end of the line. "Steve?"

"Yes?" he answered quickly.

"It was really nice of you to call," she said. "I mean, I thought about calling you to wish you good luck, but I didn't. You did. That makes you a real friend, and I want you to know I appreciate it."

"Hey, don't mention it." There was more silence as the two of them thought furiously about how to end the conversation.

"Well," he said at last, "I'll see you at the polls. Try and get some sleep—it's gonna be a long day."

"You, too. Good night, Steve."

"Good night."

She hung up and stared at the phone for a

few minutes. She'd almost forgotten she had company until she heard the knock on the door. "Come in," she called. Mary Ann was standing there, waiting eagerly for a report.

"What'd he say?"

"Just called to wish me luck," Carole said noncommittally. "You know, one of those last-minute political maneuvers. Didn't mean anything."

Mary Ann looked at her friend skeptically. Her final comment of the evening said it all: "Horsefeathers!"

Chapter Twelve

The school parking lot was practically deserted when Carole got there at eight o'clock the following morning. But over to the side she could see Steve's old VW Beetle sitting under the shade of a big tree. She pedaled over, and he rolled down the window.

"Hi," Steve said, grinning.

"How are you this morning?"

"Better now that you're here."

She walked her bike over to the rack and chained it, while he locked up his car. Then together they walked inside Twain High School and slowly made their way down the hall to the auditorium.

The election committee had worked hard the day before. The room was festooned with colored streamers and balloons. The banner across the stage read: Congratulations to the New Officers.

Along one wall were the voting booths, their doors all standing open. Somebody a few years back had come up with the bright notion of buying some cheap cardboard standing closets to use as voting booths. The tops were open to let in light and air, and they had folding doors for privacy. Each one had a piece of plywood to be used as a writing desk attached to the wall and a closed box with a slot in it for the ballots.

"You guys are early," John Haynes called from the back of the room. "If you wait a sec, I'll give you ballots, and we can get started. Of course, I could fill them out for you," he said kiddingly, "but that's not the democratic way."

"Right," Steve said, giving Carole's hand a sympathetic squeeze before starting over toward the booths. "Might as well get this over with."

John handed them each a ballot slip, and they solemnly entered two of the little cubicles and closed the doors. Carole stood there, breathing hard, gripping the stub of the pencil that would help decide her fate that day. She scanned the piece of paper and read down it. The names were ordered alphabetically, so hers was at the bottom. She felt about as low as her ranking on the ballot, but she gulped and made a big X beside her own name. Crossing her fingers for luck, she dropped the piece of paper in the box. Done. All finished. She stepped out of the booth to find Steve waiting for her.

"Well, good luck to you two," John said cheerily, turning his attention to the kids who'd just walked in the door of the auditorium. Sally Scott was at the head of the pack.

Steve nearly dragged Carole outside. They passed both Pete and Spike and gave them encouraging waves.

"Well," Carole murmured, looking nervously behind her as she and Steve rushed toward the front door, "at least everyone's voting."

"Be grateful for something," Steve said. "Hey, what are you doing this weekend?"

"What?" Carole turned to him, astonished.

"I wondered if you were busy—like all day Sunday or something?" His eyes gazed into hers, and she was lost in them, happily plunging down into the well of kindness and caring she saw there.

"Steve, I . . . I'd love to see you." Then she bit her lip. "Oh, no, but Plant Life is playing at Ellen's aunt's church bazaar. We have to set up pretty early, and then we're doing two sets."

"Great." Steve smiled, putting an arm around her shoulder and drawing her close. "I'll be there cheering you on. I've never heard you guys play— that'll be primo."

She shook her head in amazement. "I didn't think you used slang words."

"I didn't used to do a lot of things," he said. "I was pretty uptight. How'd you ever stand me?"

"Me? But I was a real nut. I must have made your life miserable. Always going on about how terrible adults were and—" She laughed and looked up at him, feeling a familiar and not unpleasant crick in her neck.

"I think we were both a mess," Steve told her. "But we're greatly improved now."

Just then, there was a yell, and Dave ran up to them. "Hey, good morning," he called.

"Hi, Dave." Carole glanced down at her watch. "I've never seen you so early before."

"Yeah, well, I had to vote, didn't I?" he asked coolly. "Had to do my duty as a citizen."

"Right," Steve said, smiling. "You were smart to beat the crowds."

Dave went inside, pulling his cap down over his eyes as though he didn't want to be recognized as somebody who'd actually gotten to school early to vote.

"He's turned around, too," Carole told Steve softly.

"Good guy, great mind," Steve said emphatically.

As more and more students started streaming into the school, Steve and Carole found themselves surrounded by well-wishers. They had little chance to talk privately. Then the first bell rang, signalling the start of the school day. "Uh—oh. Well, I guess we should go to class," Carole murmured reluctantly.

"Guess so. Meet me at the auditorium at two-fifteen, will you?" Steve asked, a look of mild panic crossing his face.

"If I haven't fainted by then," Carole said, then chuckled.

"You? Hey, you're taking this better than I am." He sighed and led her back into the corridor. Kids were milling around, talking and laughing. Some of them nodded to the two candidates, who were holding hands.

"See you later," Carole muttered, still clutching his hand.

"Can't be soon enough for me." With a look that told her exactly how much he needed and wanted her company, he pried his fingers from hers and walked away quickly.

The day crawled along. Carole meandered from class to class, her mind on voting, on Steve, on being president, on Steve, on losing the election, and on going out with Steve. They had a date for this Sunday! He was going to take her to the bazaar and watch Plant Life perform, and afterward they could talk and have something to eat and who knew what else! The nicest part was that it had been so easy. No fuss, just let's go out, poof, there they were together again. Things could only get better from here on.

By two-fifteen Carole was about to jump out of her skin. She raced from English to the auditorium, thankful that she was excused from the final period of the day because she was a candidate. She had gym, anyway, so it was an extra treat to be let out of it. When she arrived at the auditorium, panting, there was Steve, leaning on the doorframe, waiting for her. His face was kind of gray.

"Well, they're counting," he said. He licked his lips and nodded to Spike, who was lumbering toward them down the hall. Michael, Connie, and Bobby were just walking up from the other direction.

"Oh, boy, is my stomach knotted up," Carole said.

"Well, it's one of you guys," Spike said glumly. "I heard Max tell Pete that it was a tight race, but I think he was being nice." He looked at the floor, embarrassed.

"Hey," Carole told him fiercely, "nothing's decided yet. Don't give up!"

Steve smiled at her, admiring her concern for another candidate.

"What's going on?" Pete walked up behind them. "I hope their adding machines are functional." He was busily punching numbers into his own pocket calculator to ease his nerves.

"Less than an hour now." Steve looked through the open door. The election committee was busily tabulating the votes.

"I think I have to sit down," Connie said,

staggering shakily into the auditorium and plopping herself down in the back row. The others, taking her lead, selected seats nearby. Steve and Carole sat together, holding hands, waiting. The silence in the big room was oppressive.

At 3:05 exactly, John Haynes put his pencil down at the front of the room. "Got it," they heard him say.

"Oh, I can't stand this," Carole muttered, scrunching down in her seat.

"It's over, Carole." Steve put an arm around her comfortingly and whispered, "I bet you got it."

"No, it was you," she insisted, watching John saunter out of the auditorium, bound for the microphone of the public address system in Dr. Larkin's office. Another Twain High tradition was that the results were broadcast all over the school as soon as the vote was counted, and whoever chose to could stick around to hear the results. Of course, mostly everyone did. Carole sat back and shut her eyes, unable to imagine the consequences of victory or defeat. All she really was aware of now was Steve's arm, lying lightly across her shoulders.

"Everybody ready?"

Carole's eyes popped open to see Sally, looking as fresh as though she'd just stepped out of a shower. Much to Carole's dismay, Sally sat down beside them.

"I just want you to know," she murmured, "that it's been great fun running against you guys."

Carole couldn't say a word because at that instant the PA system crackled to life and John's voice boomed right in her ear.

"The vote has been counted," he announced. "I know that all Twain's senior class officers are going to do a terrific job, and I wish them well. OK! Starting with the position of treasurer, the person who'll be filling that office next year is— Pete Kelly."

Pete nodded as if he already knew, and the other candidates smiled approvingly. Steve reached over and extended his hand. "Congratulations," he said.

Then John's voice spoke again. "And for secretary, it's Steve Landy."

"Oh, my gosh!" Carole stared at him, her mouth dropping open in surprise.

Steve looked puzzled, but not terribly unhappy. "If I'm secretary," he whispered, "I'll bet you must be—"

"The new vice-president of the senior class," John's voice cut in, "is Carole Weiss."

Carole slid down in her seat, oblivious to the clapping and foot stomping of the others. She was dumbfounded—completely flabbergasted. She was happy; she was disgruntled; she was delirious. Vice-president! Yikes!

"And finally, last but certainly not least, the president. You guessed it, folks," John's voice sang out. "It's Sally Scott."

Sally jumped up, clapping her hands together in delight. She turned to give Carole's hand a quick pat, and then she went dashing out of the room, probably to go see her friends and claim the congratulations of the crowd.

"Boy, is that weird," Steve murmured as he and Carole got up to leave. "Sally for president and you for vice-president. Maybe you'll agree on one thing during the entire year."

"Really!" Carole nodded. Then she turned to him and grasped both his hands. "Are you OK? You really wanted to win this."

"Hey," Steve said and shrugged. "Forget about it. We're still right up there on top."

Carole nodded, relishing the sensation of Steve's large hand encompassing hers. They walked out the door of the auditorium and were greeted by shrieks and shouts.

"Oh, Carole!" Mary Ann threw her arms around her pal and hugged her tight. "This is the best! Honest, it couldn't have worked out better!" She sneaked a meaningful glance at Steve over Carole's shoulder. "I'm really happy for you, too, Steve," she said.

"Thanks." He turned to his friend Max, who was standing beside Mary Ann. "Well, old buddy, we can't win 'em all, huh?"

"True." Max pushed his glasses up on his nose, looking more owlish than ever. "But not being top doesn't mean you won't have any political influence at all. Actually, the slate is well-divided, and your various constituencies will be able to get ideas through at least part of the time. It's all part of the process." He nodded wisely, reaching over to shake Carole's hand. "Congratulations," he said warmly.

"Thank you, Max." Carole was instantly whirled away by a group of enthusiastic Plant Life musicians.

"Ooh, I'm so excited for you, Carole," shrieked Ellen.

"Really super," Alice said.

"I knew you were going to do it," Janice added confidently.

Carole glanced over at the huge crowd surrounding Sally, who was taking all the praise in stride. She was nodding and talking with everyone at once, but didn't seem rushed or pressured. The ultimate president, Carole had to concede. It took her several minutes to notice Dave, who was waiting quietly in a corner. She went over to him and took his outstretched hand.

"Not bad, Carole," he said earnestly. "I didn't think you had much of a chance, but I voted for you anyhow."

"I knew I could twist your arm," she teased. "Didn't hurt much, did it?"

He waggled one hand in the air dubiously. "Hey, you call me a cynic, but I knew the majority would go for more dances and cheaper yearbooks. This idealism stuff is a little over their heads, is how I figured it, so I had to throw in my two cents. This way you and Scott can argue over policy making, and Landy can decide the outcome."

"Sounds fair," she murmured, looking around to see where Steve was. She could make out his head towering over the group of kids congratulating him, and when he caught her eye, he waved and pointed toward the door.

"Your boyfriend wants to split. Well, see you." Dave pulled his cap down on his forehead.

"Dave!" she called after him. "Coming to the bazaar Sunday to catch Plant Life's debut?"

"I'll be there," he said, grinning. "Glad to see you thinking about *real* life now that this voting stuff is over." He walked away, whistling a silly little tune, and Carole fought her way through the throng surrounding Sally to get to Steve.

"Whew! Let's get out of here," he whispered in her ear.

"Don't you think we should stick around and greet our public?" she asked anxiously, as he led her down the corridor.

"Let Sally do it." He smiled confidently. "After all, she's president." Then he scooted her out the back door and around the side of the school building. It was a beautiful May afternoon. And when Steve put his arms around her and drew her into a bear hug, she realized she was probably the happiest girl in Hartford, Connecticut.

"I wonder what the vote count was," Carole said, looking up into his eyes. "It'd be interesting to know how close we were."

"The only important thing," Steve said softly, stroking her dark hair, "is how close we are right now." And then he bent down and kissed her gently on the lips.

On Sunday at the church bazaar, Steve, Dave and Max put Sally Scott's supporters to shame. They whistled and applauded after each number. Plant Life played as though they were the opening act for the Stones. But what was better was that their enthusiasm was infectious. Even the adults in the audience enjoyed Plant Life's music, particularly Carole's original song, "Be My Guy."

Carole was positively glowing when she took her bow and jumped offstage. Steve was right there in front of her when she bounded into the audience, and he folded her in his arms and whirled her off the floor.

"You were fantastic!" he yelled over the din in the church basement. "Really pro work, Carole."

"Glad you liked it," she said, grinning.

"Hey, it's really hot in here. What about some fresh air?" he suggested.

"Good idea." Together they pushed their way through the crowd and walked up the steps into the sunlight.

"I don't know how you ever had time to do all that rehearsing what with the election and all," Steve marveled.

"Well, the girls got on my case when I didn't concentrate. I was pretty distracted," Carole admitted. She wanted to tell him that it hadn't just been the campaigning on her mind all those weeks, that it had been him, too. But she just couldn't say that.

"I guess I was a little unfocused myself," Steve told her, looking at the ground. "You know, much as I wanted to be president, I had a hard time wanting to beat you. I suppose I'm not ruthless enough when it comes right down to it."

"Me either." Carole laughed.

"Hey, Carole?" He still wasn't looking at her, and he seemed to be very embarrassed about something.

"Yes?"

"I owe you an apology. It was a long time back, but I've had ample opportunity to go over the argument in my mind. I know now that you were right. I mean, if Twain High's senior class can have not only a woman president, but a woman vice-président, too, I guess the time isn't too far away when our country will have them. And I'm sure they'll do the job as well as any man. Maybe better," he finished in a rush. His face was bright red, and Carole knew how difficult it had been for him to get the apology out.

"Well, listen," she said graciously, "we were both wrong about a lot of things. I mean, I thought you were the most opinionated person in the world, but I realize now that I was just as bad. I never gave you a chance. I was a real jerk," she added in an undertone.

He tilted her face up, and she had that old familiar feeling looking up at him. "I think we have a lot going for us, Carole," he said softly. "I think neither of us won because our attentions were sort of divided these past few weeks. Mine was, anyhow. I just couldn't get you out of my mind."

Then it was Carole's turn to blush. "I used to pretend I was talking to you when I made my speeches. I suppose it sounds silly, but I had more conviction in my voice because it wasn't just a sea of faces in front of me—it was your face."

They walked along together by the border of flowers surrounding the church, holding hands and letting the things they'd just confided sink in. Suddenly Steve stopped and threw back his head in a happy laugh.

"What's so funny?" Carole asked.

"Us. Now nobody'll think it's at all weird for us to be spending every free minute together. You know, the VP and secretary just naturally have to confer on a lot of stuff. I'll tell you the truth—I was afraid to run against you because I thought it would drive us further apart, and I've been trying to think of a way to make up with you for months."

"You have? You were?" Carole was touched by his honesty, but she was even happier to realize that she had felt the same way all along. It had just taken her longer to see it. "Steve, it's incredible, really. That's what happened to me. I mean, I wanted to win very badly, but not if it meant losing you. I mean, not getting you back. I mean. . . ."

"I know what you mean, you nut!" he laughed, planting a kiss on her nose. "So it's a good thing that fate threw us back together, since we were too inept to do it ourselves."

"Uh-uh," she corrected him. "Not fate, just a fair vote count."

"And Sally's brilliant campaign strategy. Hey, wait a sec—I just want to get this straight. I'm not going to discuss school politics with you all the time."

"I should hope not," Carole declared, her hands on her hips and a broad smile on her face. "Listen, Janice is waving at me. I've got another set to do, and then I'm yours for the rest of the afternoon."

"Not just the afternoon," he whispered, dragging her out of the sunlight to a secluded corner. "Be my girl again, Carole. I love you."

"I love you, Steve," she murmured, just before he bent down to kiss her. She slid her arms around his neck and felt the sweetness of his embrace pour down over her, so that she was loose in his arms and just as delirious as a girl in love could ever be. She returned his kiss fiercely, understanding that this new relationship with Steve in a way made her more independent, not less. She was grown-up enough now to want to be his girlfriend and to forget about being his adversary.

As they drew apart, she gazed into his eyes and saw that he looked just as dreamy as she was. "I guess," she said, sighing, "that sometimes when you don't win, you do win."

"And you know what else?" Steve said, draping an arm around her and leading her back into the crowded bazaar. "Sometimes the motto 'Divide and conquer' applies to lots of things— not just school elections."

Carole agreed happily, snuggling closer into his arms. It occurred to her that the democratic process was a truly wonderful thing, especially as it applied to people. They could have their differences, fight and make up, and not compromise their principles, at least not too much.

"So," Steve said, as they approached the door and the dozens of other people, "are you ready to make music?"

"Am I ever!" she said, grinning. And then, right in front of everybody, she pulled him down for another kiss. What existed between them was the real prize, and for Carole, it meant more than winning any election. She might have lost the presidency, but together, she and Steve had won something much more precious—a victory of the heart.

Read these great new *Sweet Dreams* romances, on sale soon:

☐ **#40 SECRETS by Anna Aaron (On sale May 15, 1983 • 23510-9 •$1.95)**

—Ginny falls for Hal the first time she sees him. But though their dates are lots of fun, she can't tell how he really feels about her. And even after she lets his pet boa constrictor go for a stroll on her arm, Hal won't open up. Does he like her or doesn't he?

☐ **THE SWEET DREAMS BEAUTIFUL HAIR BOOK by Courtney DeWitt (On sale May 15, 1983 • 23375-0 • $1.95)**

—If your hair sometimes seems like your worst enemy, don't despair. Whether it's thick or thin, curly or straight, fine or coarse, blond or brunette—or somewhere in between—THE SWEET DREAMS BEAUTIFUL HAIR BOOK has all the secrets to help you stop fighting your hair—and start flaunting it.

Buy these books at your local bookstore or use this handy coupon for ordering:

SAVE $2.00 ON YOUR NEXT BOOK ORDER!

BANTAM BOOKS

Shop-at-Home Catalog

Now you can have a complete, up-to-date catalog of Bantam's inventory of over 1,600 titles—including hard-to-find books. And, you can save $2.00 on your next order by taking advantage of the money-saving coupon you'll find in this illustrated catalog. Choose from fiction and non-fiction titles, including mysteries, historical novels, westerns, cookbooks, romances, biographies, family living, health, and more. You'll find a description of most titles. Arranged by categoreis, the catalog makes it easy to find your favorite books and authors and to discover new ones.

So don't delay—send for this shop-at-home catalog and save money on your next book order.

Just send us your name and address and 50¢ to defray postage and handling costs.